THE COLORADO KILLER

KILLER

Covert

Breanna Hicks

ISBN-13: 9798361294848
ISBN-10: 1477123456

Edited by Amber McGinnis (Editor and Manager)
Cover design by: Art Painter and Canva
Library of Congress Control Number: 2018675309
Printed in the United States of America

CONTENTS

THE COLORADO KILLER

Sunday, June 14

The music is loud and drowns out my thoughts. I would love to have another drink, but I must stay attentive. It was not long ago that I was almost caught. It was the closest I have come to being noticed. Hell, I am surprised Liam even recognized me. After ten years of going unnoticed he finally saw me. It took me attacking his precious girlfriend, but he saw me. It was more satisfying than I could have imagined, him seeing me take everything he loved just as he took everything from me. Letting Liam live was a last-minute decision. I originally planned to kill the three of them; Liam, Charlotte, and her beautiful sister Darlene. But seeing Liam's face when he was holding Charlotte's unconscious body as her breathing became more and more shallow, I knew letting him live with the pain of losing another love was better than death.

As much as I hated it, I decided to leave Missouri and not return to Colorado. Having Liam see me made me want to go back to where it all started. But I also knew I could not go back to Atlanta. My parents would surely find out I was back, and they would just get in the way. I figured the beaches of Alabama were close enough. But I enjoyed the new name I earned, The Colorado Killer. It ensures that my work will be seen and remembered. That *I* will be seen and remembered for years to come. The once invisible man, seen and on the FBI's most wanted? What more could I want? I had to think of a way I could continue the Colorado Killer legacy although no longer in Colorado. So I devised a plan; I would sign all my work. Just as a hunter must tag his kill, I will tag mine.

I can only hope that Liam tracks me once again so I might continue to frame him for all my kills a little longer. One day I will show myself, when I am good and ready. One day when I am too old to hunt as easily and lure my prey; but not too old where I cannot enjoy the fame. Until then, I will hide in plain sight.

I lean back against the patio bar and take in all the beautiful women dancing and drinking. Not a care in the world. I question why I never moved to the beach sooner. This is the easiest hunting ground with new tourists to choose from every week. Women who are looking to get away, get drunk, and get laid. I can make their wildest dreams come true and they can make mine. I feel my lips curl in a devious smile as I think of all the ways.

Scanning the dance floor, I search for my 15th victim. Technically, I have a woman back home waiting for me, but I am not quite ready to end her. I could use a good kill though to fill me while I work on her a bit more.

Then I see her. Dancing with her friends, a frozen fruit cocktail in one hand with the other raised in the air. Her long chestnut hair curled to perfection. And in a tight green dress that brought out the color of her eyes even from across the room. I had to have her. In more ways than one. And not just because of her beauty, but because of what she reminded me of. The moment all those years ago and the reason I became The Colorado Killer.

CHAPTER 1: FIONA

Sunday, June 14

The air is thick and the music is loud. The patio bursts with college students on summer break. I cannot turn around without bumping into one of them. Normally I would be annoyed with all the yuppies but not tonight. No, tonight I hardly notice them. This next week is all about me and I am not going to let one more person take away my happiness.

I even treated myself to new highlights after the school year ended just for this weekend. Now, one would assume I have spent the last 3 months on the beach rather than just arriving today. My sister, Jozlynn, and I did a little shopping also where I found the perfect outfits for a week at the beach. This skin-tight emerald dress happens to be one of them. It is not my usual style but I feel sexy as hell in it and that is all that matters this week. For the next seven days, I am no longer a school teacher from Missouri; I am a single woman whose only responsibility is to have a great time.

"This is going to be the best week ever!" Eden shouts over the music.

"Yes!" I scream, raising my glass in the air as I let the alcohol and music consume me.

Leaning over, Eden asks, "I'm going to get me a refill, you want one?"

"Sure. Get me another Amaretto Sour. Frozen this time though."

I watch as Eden walks towards the bar. She is beautiful, pristine-like with the perfect blonde, a-line bob haircut, and those hourglass curves all the guys like. But I personally think she tries too hard to get their attention. And even stirs up jealousy from other girls. The way she walks with a bounce, making her hips swing more than usual, then how she sticks her rear out as she leans over the bar. I cannot help but huff as the guy next to her does not attempt to hide his appreciative stares. Normally I would feel annoyed about how slutty Eden pretends to be; how fake she becomes in public. As if she does not wear elastic scrubs everyday to work with no make-up. Tonight though, I brush off her ploys. If she wants to strut herself and have one-night stands with strange men, that is her business. I have too much on my mind to worry about her now.

For starters, I keep telling myself this will be the

perfect birthday week. The only thing that would make it better is if Charlotte were here to celebrate with me. However, she is laid up in a coma back in Kansas City. Even if she were awake, I do not know if she would want to spend the week with me after I stabbed her in the back by stealing Sawyer from her. But if I would not have got Sawyer to call off their wedding, she would be married to a prick. I do not even understand how she stayed with him for the two years that she did, I could barely stand him for the four months we were officially together.

Instead, Charlotte went off to Colorado and met a dreamy mountain man. I only saw Liam once when I went to visit her in the hospital but she definitely got lucky with that one. Then again, if she would have gone on her honeymoon with Sawyer, she would not have crossed paths with the Colorado Killer and she would not be in a coma today. So did I save her, or am I the reason she is fighting death every single day?

Eden snaps me out of my thoughts when she returns with our drinks. "Oh my goodness, Fiona. You will not believe who I just met at the bar. I think he could be the one. He is so mysterious and was totally playing hard to get."

'Do you even know where he lives? He could live all the way across the country for all you know. Do you really want to start something long-distance like that?' This is what I want to say. Instead, I simply ask, "Oh yeah? Are you going to go back up there and talk to him more?" Eden has this belief that every guy wants her and if they breathe in her general direction, they are Mr. Right. I have learned to indulge her, knowing that by the night's end, he will leave and she will never see him again. Or a better Mr. Right will come along, making her forget the first guy ever existed.

I sneak a glance at the bar and see the same guy who stared at Eden's backside leaning against the bar and staring in our direction. He is kind of handsome I will admit. He has the complete beach vibe going on and I do have a thing for men with shaggy hair.

"Hey, guys. Where did Alice run off to?" Jozlynn interrupts as she joins us back on the dance floor.

"She probably went for a walk down by the beach or something. You know this isn't her scene since having Iris." Alice used to go out with Jozlynn and me all the time growing up. But ever since she married Aaron and had a baby last year, she quit joining us. Even this weekend was like pulling teeth to get her to take a vacation and let loose. Not like she is doing a lot of relaxing. Alice has not gone more than five minutes without FaceTiming or texting Aaron.

"Well, she is the one missing out. If she wants to

spend the whole week alone on the beach, so be it." Eden chirps as she dances away, making herself more in view of the stranger at the bar.

I use this moment to steal a second glance at Eden's newest Mr. Right still sitting at the bar. The next thing I know, I am locking eyes with him. Typically, I would pay her love interests no attention, as they are your average womanizers. But not this one. He portrays self-assurance as if he is the hottest guy here tonight. But he also has a quiet, mysterious vibe that draws me in. I am instantly captivated by the depth of his honey-brown eyes. When he looks at me, I feel as though he is seeing right through to my core. I am not sure if I should feel disturbed by this but I cannot help but like the notion of being fully seen for once.

Our connection is broken as Eden purposely bumps into Mr. Right as she pretends to be drunker than she really is. We call this the classic Eden move. And for reasons beyond me, it always ends with the guy asking for her number or taking her to the bathroom and screwing her right there in the stall. To my surprise, it does not work on this Mr. Right. Which just intrigues me more. What man in a bar, at the beach, on summer break, turns down a drunk girl looking to get laid?

'*Who is this man?*' I ask myself.

CHAPTER 2: LIAM

Thursday, April 16

Charlotte has been in a coma for almost three days now. The doctors do not know what is wrong with her. Or that is what they are telling me anyway. All day long it is nothing but a revolving door of doctors and nurses. Taking vitals, changing her IV bag, and checking and repacking her wounds. No matter what they are doing, they always end the same; they look up from Charlotte, make eye contact with me, and give me a look of pity. They really need to work on their empathetic faces and bedside manner.

"So doc," I holler as I chase after the latest doctor, "what is going on with Charlotte? It has been almost three weeks and no one is telling me anything."

She slowly turns around with a look of dread for having to talk to me. "Are you family?" She asks directly.

I'm, um. I'm her..." I trail off, not sure what I am exactly. "No, I'm not."

"Then I am sorry sir, but I have nothing to tell you." And with that, the doctor turns on her heel to walk away. But before she takes another step, she turns back and with a softer voice tells me, "Look, sir, I truly am sorry. I wish I could tell you more. But hospital policy is you have to be family. What I can say is, if you are a praying man, I would start praying. That girl needs a miracle."

The next few minutes are a blur as I try to process the news. The hospital staff around me become a haze as the noise turns to murmurs like I am underwater. When I finally blink back to reality, I remember Charlotte's sister, Darlene, was brought to this hospital also. She must know what the doctors are saying. I rush to the nurses' station to inquire what room Darlene is in.

Knocking on the door, "Darlene? May I come in?"

Darlene looks over from her show on TV and uses what strength she has to nod.

"My name is Liam. I was there at the hardware store when umm.." I stop, not ready to say the words aloud.

"I remember. Please, sit down." She instantly perks up with a wave of strength as she recognizes me. "So you know my sister?"

"We met in Colorado when she was there a couple of weeks ago." Did she really not tell her sister about me? I suppose she thought it best to keep me a secret. If only it would have been enough to protect them.

"Wait. You're *that* Liam? The one from the news wanted for all those murders?"

News travels fast I suppose, even false news. "The FBI did question me but I promise you, I am not the Colorado Killer. But I know who is, and I think I'm responsible."

"You know the man who killed all those people? You have to say something."

"The man who kidnapped you, who held you hostage-"

"That was the Colorado Killer? The same guy who kidnapped me and put Charlotte in a coma is the same one who committed those murders? Why did he let us-" Before she can get the question out, she has a new realization. "Wait, this serial killer is still out there somewhere and you are just sitting here? He is probably stalking his next victim. Or worse, what if he knows Charlotte and I survived? What if he tries to come back and finish the job?"

Ignoring her incessant questions, I finish my sentence. "-his name is Jack. He works at the Convenience Store back in Redbrook. Or at least he did. I don't know where he is now. I always thought he was kind of odd, but I never would have pegged him as the killer type. And I do not have the slightest clue why he pointed the FBI in my direction."

"But you said you think you are responsible? Knowing a psycho doesn't make you responsible. And neither does a psycho trying to pin you for their murders. You didn't make him kidnap me or attack Charlotte did you?"

"No, but right before he knocked me out, he said something. He said I stole something from him, so he is taking Charlotte from me." In a quieter tone, I go on. "If I would not have fallen for Charlotte, she would never have crossed his path. Both of you would be home safe right now." I slink back in my chair as I let all the regret consume me.

"How did you meet my sister?" It is not the question I thought she was going to ask. "And why did she not tell me about you when she got back?"

I decide it is better, and safer, for Darlene to know the truth so I tell her everything. The blizzard, the near bear attack, even how I fell in love with Charlotte in the firelight.

"Charlotte wanted to tell you," I explained. "But she knew if you knew the truth, it would put a target on your back. What we did not expect was Jack to follow her home and attack you anyway. We expected if he followed anyone, he would follow me.

I mean, I'm the one he has been framing for all those murders. I'm the one he has a problem with. I guarantee if Charlotte, even myself, if we would have known Jack would follow her, we would have told you the truth. We were trying to protect you."

Darlene was silent. Time seems to stop as she processes what I said. When she does get her thoughts together to speak, I have to replay her words. "Well Liam, you are right. If you would not have met her, she would not have become the Colorado Killer's next intended victim." She pauses for a moment as the words sink deep. "But she would have died in that blizzard, whether from the frigid weather or the bear. Either way, she still would not be home safe in her own bed. So don't blame yourself. Way I see it, you saved her in Colorado and you saved us both in that hardware store. Hell, from here, it seems as though she may have saved you also."

I can not believe what Darlene is saying. These last two years people have told me Rebecca's death was not my fault. But I never believed those words until now. This time it was different. I know Darlene is right. If I would not have met Charlotte when I did, she would most likely be dead instead of in a coma five doors down.

I sit with Darlene a little longer as she tells me more about Charlotte and her childhood growing up. I never knew Charlotte was a baseball fan. In college, she even snuck into the team's after-party when the Indians won the College World Series. I knew she was feisty but never would have pegged her for the devious rule-breaker type. I wish I would have known her back then, I think she would have set my whole life on a different trajectory. For instance, I would never have taken Rebecca up on her dare that led to me taking her out for a drink. Maybe I would never have earned the attention of a serial killer. And then Charlotte and I would be living our life right now, not fighting for her life or always looking over my shoulder.

Back in Charlotte's room, I scoot my chair close to her bedside as I start to weep. A million thoughts race through my mind, the first being how can a burly man like myself be weeping like a middle school girl whose crush just went to the dance with her best friend. Other thoughts come flooding in as I think about what I could have done, what I should have done, differently. I should not have let her come back to Kansas City alone. I should not have been such a coward to go hide and leave Charlotte.

"Charlotte," I trail off. "I'm sorry. I should have been there for you sooner. I should never have let you out of my sight. It's true what your family is saying, you would have been better off if I never would have brought you to my cabin. If I would have taken you to the hospital that night instead. But -" Speaking more to myself, I continue as the words flow out of my mouth before I realize what I am saying. "I know I wouldn't have been." I stop when I hear the words. How can I be so selfish at a time like this?

Accepting the truth, I speak to Charlotte again. This time with confidence. "I would not trade our week in Colorado for never having met you. No, what I should have done was realize Jack was a killer sooner. All those times I went into the convenience store or saw him getting his morning coffee at Mama's Diner, I should have known he was a sociopath. I brushed off his impersonal demeanor as being socially awkward when actually it was his lack of empathy blocking his ability to connect with others. But what did he mean I took something from him?" I sit back in my chair as I ponder Jack's claim and process aloud to myself. "The Colorado Killer killed his first victim in Atlanta. It all started with Rebecca. Before her, he simply robbed houses when their owners were out."

I sat there in silence next to Charlotte as I let the memories of Atlanta come back. I have locked them away for so long, willing myself to leave that life and everything with it behind. I first met Rebecca in college at Valdosta State. I was out with some buddies after a long week of midterms when out of nowhere, this girl approached me at the bar. She started with small talk about the ambience and the wannabe freshman kids there, those too young to drink but still wanting to fit in. She even made me a bet that these two guys would chug their mocktails then try to hit on a couple of senior girls partying on the other side of the bar. She was cute and seemed friendly so I took her up on the bet. I lost of course and had to buy her the next round. But that night I believed I was the real winner as I watched her walk back to her table, holding a napkin in my hands that she used to write down her phone number. That is when it hit me. I was too preoccupied watching the sway of her hips to notice the man sitting at the table glaring back at me. Rebecca was there on a date with another guy. I focused my mind to look past her and as the guy came into view, there he was, Jack. That night in the bar, nine years ago, I took Rebecca right out from under him. And now, Charlotte is paying the price.

Just as the thought of Charlotte's payment crosses my mind, her alarms start going off. She is failing. And it is all my fault.

CHAPTER 3: THE COLORADO KILLER

Monday, June 15

I watch my latest haul through the computer screen in my hidden private office upstairs. When I found myself in Alabama, I had two stipulations to rent a house. First, it needed land. I did not want to get interrupted in my endeavors by some nosey neighbors. Second, the land needed to have an underground wine cellar *'because being the wine aficionado that I am, I need a dark, temperature controlled room to store my expensive wines.'* Or at least that is what I told the Landlord. Truth is, I hate wine. It is just too dangerous to have my haul upstairs for anyone to happen upon by accident. That and the neighbors are less likely to hear commotion when it is below ground. And this house, set back behind abandoned shacks along the beach, was the perfect place.

Although I have a beautiful catch right in front of me to keep me occupied, I cannot stop thinking about Her. The way pieces of her hair shaped her face and draped over her shoulder. The way the emerald dress hugged her curves and brought out the hues of her eyes. I decided last night to let her go for now. Simply killing her would be too easy. And with the memories she brings me, I want to make her my best hunt yet.

Not being able to take it any longer, I lock up my office and head back to The Oasis Patio Bar & Grill, leaving the woman in my cellar to live another night. There is no guarantee this other woman will be there but I figure the bar where I saw her last night is a good place to begin.

At the bar, I make a couple of rounds around the patio to no avail. Finishing off my Jack and Coke, I decide to try the next bar down the beach. But as soon as I reach the door, there she is. The woman in the emerald dress, yet this time, she is in a bright orange mini skirt, highlighting her fake tan.

There is no time to plan a charming introduction, so instead, I settle with a simple and polite, "Hi" Although it comes out more awkward than casual.

"Oh, hello!" she responds in a tone so light-hearted and smooth that it nearly takes my breath away. She would have taken it too if women actually had that hold over me. After Rebecca left me in that bar for Liam, I swore to myself not another person would get me all tied up the way Rebecca once did. Yet here she is, standing right in front of me, getting me all tied up with one bat of the eye after another.

"I don't mean to be brazen, but you were in here last night weren't you?"

Luckily she did not find my question too forward as she answers, "Yeah, I was here with some friends last night. We just got in town."

"I thought I recognized you. You looked stunning in that green dress."

"You remember what dress I was wearing? I expected you to be too busy with Eden to have noticed me, let alone remember my outfit."

So she does recognize me. "I'm not sure I know who Eden is, but anyone in this bar last night noticed you. I can guarantee you that."

"Eden is one of my friends that I was here with last night. The girl you were talking to practically all night. She was disappointed when she couldn't get you to dance with her, you know. Especially when the song *Girls Just Wanna Have Fun* came on. That is her song." She finishes her last remark with a sort of skeptical laugh and there she went, giving me another twist around her finger.

"Oh right. Well, we're here now and I don't see her around anywhere." I prod, looking around her. "Can I buy you a drink?" For a moment, I think I pushed my luck a little too far as she stares at me with a mistrustful look in her eyes. "Just one drink. If you're not enjoying my company after that, you're free to go. No questions asked."

And there was that smile. The one that creates the one dimple and squints her eyes. *'I'm in.'*

"Give me a Jack and Coke and an Amaretto Sour?" I order. Remembering almost too late that trustful people use manners, I quickly add, "Um, please?" I cannot have this beautiful prize of a woman think she cannot trust me so soon.

"Wait, you know my drink." She speaks up, more of a statement than a question.

"Oh, um. I noticed you were drinking one last night. I had a friend in college who would always drink them. Except he was a guy so we all would give him a hard time about it. So when I saw you with one, it reminded me of the good ol' days and stuck with me. Would you like something different?"

"No, an Amaretto Sour is perfect. I was just surprised, that is all. No one ever remembers my drink order."

Once again, my quick-wittedness saves my ass again.

CHAPTER 4: FIONA

Monday, June 15

'Thank you Joz!' I will have to remember to thank her when we head back to the condo. It was her idea for the two of us to go out for a quick drink while Eden and Alice stayed back to cook dinner. And she was right, this is exactly what I needed tonight. This guy, which I just realized, I do not know his name; "I'm Fiona by the way."

"Oh, sorry. Name's Jack."

Jack. I like that. Well, Jack here is laying the charm on thick. I cannot help but wonder how many times he has picked up girls at a bar. He either is a pro, knowing when and where to be observant or he has never done this before and is attempting to cover up how he feels like a fish out of water. Either way, he seems sweet enough. Not like those other guys who go from a *'what's up'* to instantly trying to get in your pants. Even Sawyer never remembered my drink. We spent a week in the Caymans and after correcting him a million times, he still ordered me a daiquiri. It is not until Jack here orders my drink right the first time that I realize just how much I instantly feel known already.

"So Jack, tell me, what brings you to Orange Beach?"

"I actually just moved here a couple of months ago. Things back home just got a little too stressful and I needed a change. And what better place to get away from the chaos than the beach, am I right?"

"I actually know exactly what you mean." I laugh. Although looking around, it does not seem very peaceful with all the people crammed into the tiny space. One cannot walk from one side to the other without feeling like they are swimming upstream.

"You say that like you're running away from something also." He inquires.

"You're right. Well, I'm hiding more than running. I'll have to go back at the end of the week unfortunately." I hesitate before continuing. "I just got out of a relationship that didn't end too well. And I didn't want to spend my birthday being reminded of what happened. So here I am."

"Well, you definitely came to the right place. Besides, that guy was an idiot for letting you go. If you were mine, I wouldn't let you out of my sight." I got a chill down my neck as Jack said those last words. I cannot quite explain why; maybe because no one has ever talked to me that way before. No one ever made me their priority.

I let out a snort, "Only if he considered that before shacking up with our scuba instructor while on our vacation." The bartender brings our drinks in perfect timing. Allowing me to distract myself with my drink instead of the guilt I feel that Sawyer cheating on me was somehow my own fault. I mean, he cheated on Charlotte with me. And he was engaged to her. Did I really expect him to go on the straight and narrow now that we were together?

"Dang. He's more of an idiot than I gave him credit for."

Once again, Jack surprises me. I am not sure what response I was expecting, but he gives me a sense of peace with those words. As if finally, someone does not blame me for letting the *perfect guy* get away.

About an hour and two drinks later, Joz sneaks her way to Jack and I at the bar. "Hey y'all. Sorry to interrupt, but Fiona, you weren't answering my texts."

Taking my phone out of my wristlet, I see 2 missed texts from Eden, 4 missed texts from Joz, and 2 missed calls. "Oh, I'm so sorry. We're having such a great time, I didn't hear it go off." I see Joz's inquisitive look and instantly know what she is asking. Joz and I have always been able to have conversations without saying a word. It used to drive our mom crazy, which caused us to do it all the more.

"Where are my manners? Jack, this is Jozlynn, my sister. Joz, this is Jack."

Jack gives a charming yet shy smile, "Hey."

"Hi Jack. It's nice to meet you. Again, I'm sorry for intruding." Turning her attention back to me, "Alice called me. Dinner is ready, so we should probably head back."

"Of course. I almost forgot. Jack, it was really nice talking to you, I had a great time tonight. But we promised our friends we would join them for dinner tonight."

"No problem. But hey, I would love to see you again. And hear more about that beach in South Carolina."

"Yeah, that sounds great. Why don't I give you my number and you can call me later."

On the walk back to the condo, Joz decides it would be fun to play 20 questions. *Where is he from? What does he do? Why did he move to Alabama? Does he have siblings? Why did he leave Atlanta?*

"Joz, give me a break. I just met the guy an hour ago."

"Well, what did y'all talk about if you didn't talk about what the guy does for a living." She whines.

"We talked about," I pause for a moment, realizing he did not say much about himself at all. "Well, he was very curious about me. He actually cared about what I was saying and listened to me rather than always turning the conversation back to him. He was very sweet and charming."

Luckily we reach the condo before she can ask anymore questions.

"Hey Joz, real quick before we go inside. Can we keep Jack between us for now? I don't feel like talking about him with Eden and Alice just yet."

"Of course FiFi. Lips are sealed."

I make my way to the patio after dinner. Eden and Alice made a phenomenal shrimp fettuccine. Blackened shrimp with a smooth butter garlic sauce and just enough tang of lemon. The first bite instantly made me melt in my chair as I took in all the flavors.

To continue the relaxing evening, I just want to sit under the stars as I listen to the ocean waves crash onto the beach. My thoughts take me back to Jack and our conversation at the bar. I have not enjoyed talking to someone that much in quite some time. I just had to go and ruin it by telling him to call me. *'Call me? Seriously Fiona? What were you thinking?'* A guy like Jack is not into the whole relationship thing and then I just had to slip and go all middle school

girl on him. I could have said anything else; text me, hit me up, anything besides call me.

Unfortunately, the tranquility of the night is quickly interrupted by Eden's shrill laughter as the girls join me on the patio. I try to be present and listen as Alice babbles on about the newest drink menu she created for her coffee shop and Eden chimes in about the hot guy she saw on her breakfast run this morning. But all I can think about is how I long to stare into Jack's dark honey eyes again.

I am about to turn in for the evening, having heard enough gossip for one night, when my phone buzzes. My heart skips a beat as a dose of dopamine surges through me and I glance down, seeing a number I do not recognize. I quickly swipe up to see if it is the text I have been waiting for. And there it is.

> *'Hey its Jack from the bar. It was great talkin to you tonight. So listen if your not doin anything tomorow night theres this great seafood joint just over in Gulf Shores. Want to go?'*

Simultaneously, I feel giddy with excitement while my teacher-side edits all his grammar and spelling errors. *'Not all of us can be literalist I suppose'*, and I attempt to brush it off as I formulate the perfect response. Not wanting to sound so mushy like I did at the bar.

After five attempts, I give up and settle on a response. *'Hey Jack. Sure, I would love to try it out. I*

am always looking for new restaurants to visit.' That will have to do, leave the ball in the guy's court this time to plan the date. I have always been the one to control and plan, it is time to let someone else take over. Then I can see how much effort he tends to put into wooing me.

As I gather my blanket and drink, I make eye contact with Joz to tell her I have a date. By her glance, I can tell she has questions amidst her excitement.

"Alright guys, I'm going to turn in for the night. Eden, Alice, thank you again for dinner. It was absolutely delicious. Now it's time for a food coma."

Joz quickly jumps up, "You know, that sounds like a great idea. We have a busy morning tomorrow, I think I will head in also." She bunches up her blanket and is on my heels in a matter of seconds. Once we reach my room, she runs in and plops down on my bed.

"Spill. Tell me everything! What did he say? Did he ask you out?"

I sit down next to her and show her the texts. "How am I supposed to leave tomorrow night? They're going to know something is up. I wouldn't just leave on my own birthday week, you know that. And you know neither of them will let me go without questions."

Joz ponders for a moment, "Well, we were talking about going to that new bar down the road further for dinner. You could say whatever you eat for lunch is not settling well for you so you want to come back to lay down and sleep it off. What do you think?"

"There's a reason mom never caught you sneaking off when we were growing up. You're too good at this."

"Well mom was also too busy fondling with Rodger to really care. But yes. I am that good." Standing up, Joz does not give me time to argue. "So it's settled then. Tomorrow, you're going to get sick after lunch, stay back when we all leave for dinner, and then you my little sis, are going to get that rebound going on."

Without saying a word, I smile and give her a hug goodnight. Once the door closes behind her, I slip out of my dress, pull on my cotton shorts, and crawl into bed where I let the downy comforter engulf me.

Three hours later, I awake to the sound of footsteps coming from the kitchen and creaking of cabinet doors opening and closing. I look at the clock on my nightstand that reads 2:00 AM. '*What in the world are they doing up at 2:00 AM still?*' I pull my covers down and swing my legs off the bed to check out what the girls are up to now. And why it requires them to be so loud. I grab my robe before opening the door and fasten it closed as I walk down the hallway to

the kitchen. But when I round the corner, there is no one there. All the lamps are turned on, as well as the light above the stove. I begin to tell myself that I must have been hearing things when I notice the drawers of the roll top desk are open. As I scan the rest of the room, that is when I see it. The sliding patio door sitting wide open, the sound of ocean waves streaming through.

I take a step back and quickly glance around, making sure whoever was in the condo was not sitting and lurking in the shadows. As soon as I was partially sure the intruder had left, I turned on my heels and ran to Jozlynn's room.

Barging in without knocking, "Joz! Wake up! Someone was in the house! Joz! Damn it Joz, wake up!"

"What?" she moans. "FiFi, what are you doing in my room?" Joz never was a light sleeper.

"There was someone in the house. The lights were on, the desk drawers opened, and the sliding glass door was wide open!" I breathlessly explain.

"Fi, it was probably just Eden or Alice. You know how forgetful Eden can get when she's been drinking. Just close the doors and go back to sleep, mmkay"

Yeah, she was still asleep and not truly listening to me. "No, Joz. You don't understand." I say, shaking her again. "I heard footsteps and someone rummaging through our cabinets. But when I

walked out to look what it was, the person was gone. Eden and Alice's lights are off in their rooms so it could not have been them. Joz, you have to wake up. Im'm serious, someone was in our house, going through our stuff!"

"Fiinnnee." She whines as she rolls out of bed and slips on her sweater.

Once in the living room, we carefully look around to make sure nothing was missing or out of place. "I don't see anything missing. Maybe I spooked them before they could take anything."

"Eh, I wouldn't speak too soon." Joz says as she fumbles through papers in the roll top desk.

"Why? What is it?"

"Wake up Eden and Alice. Now!"

After ten attempts to wake Eden from her drunken coma, all four of us are standing in the living room where I fill them in on what I heard and saw. Eden and Alice go through the same denial process that Joz did. That is until Joz speaks up.

"Guys, it's missing!"

"What's missing?" Alice asks, rubbing the sleep from her eyes.

"It. The gift." Jozlynn takes a deep breath, realizing the girls are not following. "Fiona, I made you a gift.

I was waiting for Saturday to give it to you, I wanted it to be a surprise. It's a scrapbook from all our favorite memories growing up. I know it has been a rough few weeks and I wanted to cheer you up by reminiscing about the good ol' days."

"Awe, Joz, that is so sweet of you! I love that!"

"Well, don't get too excited. Because it is missing. Whoever was in here must have taken it."

Eden speaks up; "Okay, hold on. Out of all the electronics we have lying around, our purses even, why would someone take a damn scrapbook? No offense Joz."

"Yeah, are you sure you didn't just misplace it?" Now it is Alice who is doubting Joz and me. I suppose I don't blame them. It is very strange the intruder didn't take anything more valuable. I would be skeptical also if I would not have heard them rummaging around. Hell, what intruder climbs two stories up when there are just as nice condos on the first floor?

"Listen, I don't know what makes someone break in and steal something so personable. But I know for a fact that I put it in this desk when we got here Saturday. Fiona made a grocery run so I took the opportunity and hid it. And now, it is missing. So unless one of you moved it, it did not just grow a pair of legs and walk off. Someone had to have taken it." We could all hear the annoyance growing in Joz's

voice.

And leave it to Eden to snap back. "Well then call the cops. I don't know what you think they're going to do though."

"Don't y'all feel violated?" I step in. "Some stranger was in our house. They walked right past your rooms and went through our personable belongings. Whether you think what they took is invaluable or not, I think we should call the police. If the person comes back, they would at least have a record started."

And that settles it. Joz leaves the room to fetch her cell phone and call the police. We spend the next 2 hours going over our account of the evening with the police officer. It is not until 5:00 AM that I crawl back into my cozy bed to attempt to get some rest. But everytime I close my eyes, my mind takes me somewhere I do not want to be. In our condo with the intruder. But this time, they do not stop at the desk, rather they make it to my room. I imagine I hear footsteps walking down the hallway, my bedroom door creaking open, and there standing at the edge of my bed, a masked figure. Just as they lunge towards me, I awake with a startle. Sitting straight up in bed trying to catch my breath and slow my heart.

CHAPTER 5: THE COLORADO KILLER

Tuesday, June 16

At my kitchen table, I sip on my morning coffee and flip through the scrapbook I found at Fiona's condo this morning. She was just as beautiful as a teenager as she is now. She seems to have gotten lucky and skipped past the awkward years of braces, pimples, and bad haircuts. I shudder at the memory of being a teenager. That is when the bullying started; name calling, being the butt of the jokes, even girls pretending to be interested in me just to give the boys more things to joke about. Luckily it only lasted a couple of years. Once I reached High School, I became invisible. To the point I would ping pong off the other students as they shoved past me in the hallways as if I were not even there. But at least they were leaving me alone I suppose.

Not Fiona though. No, she was beautiful enough to

be a model. According to these photos, she was a model in those Little Miss Pageants as a little girl. I will have to ask her if she ever tried competing for Miss. America. I assume she did not because if she competed, she was sure to have won, and there would be a photo of her winning in this album.

My thoughts of Fiona in an emerald sequined ball gown and tiara are quickly interrupted by the faint mumbles of the woman in the wine cellar. My newest prize's way of reminding me to stop and have a little fun before my date with Fiona tonight. I did leave her early yesterday so I owe her some of my attention today.

This woman, Laine, I met Friday night at Shoreline's. When I moved to town, it was the first place I went; I needed a little liquid xanax to relax and what better place to go than a bar. That particular day, they happened to have a *Help Wanted* sign plastered in the window. I do not have bartending experience but I have been to enough bars to know how to fake my way into making the big tips. I spoke to the manager that night and was mixing drinks the very next night.

This particular Friday night, I was serving drinks when a couple of surfer boy wannabe's were antagonizing this beautiful woman. LIke the knight in shining armor that I am, I swooped in to save this damsel. Yet, instead of accepting my heroism and my offer to buy her a drink, she barely looked at me, mumbled a heartless *'thanks'*, and walked back to her table. Her first mistake. The second was when all the girls from her table looked in my direction and laughed.

'I'll show her to reject me.' I huff as I turn the knob to the wine cellar.

"Well good evening Laine. Were you good last night?" Of course, all she could do was muffle a scream as I left the gag over her mouth. "You shouldn't have been so rude to ignore my polite gesture. I did not have to give you a free drink. I actually don't have that authority yet so it came out of my own paycheck."

I pick up a pair of pliers and spin them around a couple of times in my hand to give Laine time to squirm. "You did this, you know? You deserve this." Using the pliers, I seductively trace her neck, down her ample cleavage, and stop at her toned stomach while I retrace the pathway with my eyes. Taking in the curves of her hips, the rise and fall of her breasts as she attempts to control her breath, the sweat perspiring down her neck, her lips hugging the gag, and landing on her eyes staring back at me.

"You are lucky," I tell her. "All the others I killed right away. I have given you four more days that none of them got. You should be grateful, I didn't have to bring you back here. Every minute I don't kill you is a gift."

With that last remark, she loses any control she had left and begins screaming in between sobs. This is when I know I got her, and with a little laugh, I begin to rip out her finger nails one by one. When I get to the ninth nail, I am interrupted by my phone indicating a text. I leave Laine to catch her breath while I check who could be texting me. When I see it is Fiona, I feel my lips turn up in a smile. What is happening? I was planning to make Fiona victim number 16 but none of my previous targets have made me feel this way. I am not sure if I like it.

'Hey Jack! I'll be heading to the restaurant here soon, I'm looking forward to seeing you!'

I check the time and realize it is already half past six. I should wrap this up if I am going to meet Fiona at 7 o'clock. Setting my phone down, I look back up at Laine. I can tell as I ripped out her nails, that I ripped out all hope from her eyes along with them. I inhale deeply, letting the high consume me. But I know it will not last long. Once they lose hope, all the fun dissipates, so there is no point keeping them around.

"Laine, my dear. Take in these last few hours you have left. I have a date to get to, but when I get back, it's the end."

I leave her to cry in darkness as I head upstairs to meet Fiona for our date. But I want to make a quick stop on my way.

CHAPTER 6: FIONA

Tuesday, June 16

"Eden!" I shout from my room. We are all getting ready to go to dinner followed by a night on the town and I cannot find my shoes. However, only Jozlynn knows that I do not plan on making it to the bar. I devised a plan to fake feeling sick so I can leave the girls and meet Jack for our date. It all started shortly after lunch. I began complaining of a stomach ache so the fake illness does not just come out of nowhere.

"Eden! Do you still have my red heels? I want to wear them with my new white dress!" I shout again.

Eden walks into my room carrying my favorite red heels. "Fiona!" She exclaims. "I love that dress! It reminds me of Marilyn Monroe. You have to let me borrow it this week." Eden idolizes celebrities but Marilyn tops them all. She even cut her hair to look like hers.

"Guys, we're going to be late." Alice interrupts. "What is taking y'all so long?"

"I couldn't find my shoes. But I'm ready now, get Jozlynn and I'll meet you in the kitchen."

As we open the door to leave, we smell the stench before noticing the dead fish laying on our welcome mat with a note. Alice is the first one to gain her composer enough to pick up the letter.

"Have fun tonight ladies. Enjoy your freedom while you can. One of you might not make it back." She reads the letter aloud but it takes me reading it once more to really understand what it says.

"Okay. Is anyone else as freaked out by this as I am? Like what is this?" Eden squeals.

Alice, being the most sane one of the group steps in. "It's probably just some delinquents getting bored and being dumb. I saw a group of teenagers follow me onto the elevator the other night, they probably saw what room we were in and wanted to mess with us."

"Alice is right. I mean, it's a dead fish and a note. It's not like someone is stalking us." Jozlynn said it was nothing, but you could tell in her voice, she was trying to convince herself just as much as she was us. "We should save the note just in case though. But can someone bring me some paper towels? Lots of paper towels."

Jozlynn throws the paper towels over the fish and carefully picks it up by the tail as if she might get the stench on her if she gets too close. With her arm outstretched, she rushes to the trash at the end of the hall and flings in the fish.

"Well, now that's taken care of, can we please go eat? I'm starving!" Eden whines.

"Calm down Eden. I just touched a dead fish for goodness sake. Can I please wash my hands first? Or will you starve to death before then?"

As we walk towards the restaurant, I begin to slow my pace and rub my temples. I am no actress but I can fool people for a short while. Jozlynn, knowing what I am doing, is the first to speak up.

"Fiona, are you all right? You don't look so hot."

"I don't know what happened. I started feeling nauseous after lunch and then all of a sudden I got really lightheaded. I think that whole fish debacle got me worked up on top of lunch not settling with me."

"You're probably just hungry. I'm sure you will be fine once you eat something." You would think Eden being the nurse of the group, would have more empathy for others. But I guess she's only empathetic while on duty.

"I don't know Fiona, you look a little pale. Do you

want to sit for a moment?" Leave it to Alice to be the caring one. I mean, she is a mom. Doesn't caring for others become second nature to you once you have kids?

"I could use a break. But we have reservations, I don't want y'all to miss it. I'll just head back to the condo and lie down for a bit."

Jozlynn, being the better actress than I, "Are you sure? You were looking forward to trying this restaurant."

"Yeah, I'm sure. Y'all go on ahead. If I feel better I will meet y'all or you can bring me back something. I'll be fine, I promise." And just like that, I am headed to meet Jack in the complete opposite direction. Jozlynn was right though, I was really looking forward to trying the Seafood Gumbo. But maybe this place Jack recommended will have gumbo. It is the gulf after all.

"Wow. You look beautiful!" Jack looks at me like every girl dreams of being looked at. As if everyone else disappeared and it is only you standing there.

"Oh, thank you." I gleam. "My friend said I looked like Marilyn Monroe, but I don't think I come close to as beautiful as she was."

"Well, I would say you're way more gorgeous than she ever was." Someone is laying on the charm, but as long as he is willing to give the compliments, I will happily keep accepting them.

At our table, Jack orders our drinks as I look over the menu. They have a full list of entrees I would love to try, but I only care about finding one thing.

"They do have it!" My excitement comes out louder than I would have liked. It was supposed to stay inside my head. At least I did not yell, but it was not much of a whisper either. I try so hard to reign in my emotions; hopefully my outburst does not make Jack think I am immature or that I cannot control myself.

"What's that?" He asks calmly.

"Oh, I'm sorry about that. It's just, I have been craving seafood gumbo. They don't have a mixed seafood one, but they do have a shrimp option. It's close enough." When I look up to gauge his thoughts on my outburst, I realize he is not disgusted at all. Rather, he has a slight smile as if he enjoyed my excitement instead of it being an embarrassment to him.

We spend the rest of dinner talking about my job as a teacher back in Kansas City, my dream of visiting Europe, and what it was like growing up in Chicago. I try harder tonight to ask him questions and allow him to share about himself. Jack does talk more about his job as a bartender and how he enjoys hunting trips but he quickly turns the conversation back to me as soon as he can. Although I still do not know much about him, I really enjoy being with him and who I am when we are together. He is very romantic to care about me and he listens so intently. Most guys I date are too involved in themselves to care about anyone else.

I am too busy talking to notice the waiter drop off the check. It is not until Jack asks if I would like to take a walk to the pier that I realize he has already paid the bill.

Once we reach the beach out front of the restaurant, I blush. "I'm sorry, how rude of me. I have been talking your ear off. Tell me more about you. You mentioned earlier you go on frequent hunting trips, where was your last trip?"

"No, you're fine. I actually enjoy listening to your stories." In the same breath, he continues, "Awe, look at the dog." I follow where he is pointing to see a couple playing frisbee with their black lab.

"Oh my goodness!" I exclaim. "It is so cute! He reminds me of my dog I had growing up."

"Let me guess, a golden retriever?"

"Yes! How did you know?"

"Just a lucky guess," he smirks.

Am I really that easy to read I wonder. Do I have a 'golden retriever' personality or something? I suppose it is a popular breed. "He was the sweetest dog, Shadow. Yes, named after my favorite movie as a child, don't judge. We would take him with us to the lake and play fetch in the water. Shadow would jump in, chasing the stick, even to the bottom." I let out a little laugh as the nostalgia returned. "We even had one of those multiple room tents-"

"Oh, the orange and gray one." Jack pauses and looks at me.

"Wait, how do you know what color it was?"

"No, you just reminded me of this orange and gray tent I had as a kid also. It just had two rooms though. Definitely not as cool as yours it sounds."

Orange and gray was a popular tent color back then. I suppose it is possible he had one also. "Yeah, well Shadow had his very own bed in my room. He was quite spoiled."

I stop as we reach the end of the pier and let the quiet ambience overtake me. Taking a deep breath in, the crisp air from the ocean fills my lungs. It is times like this that make me never want to return home. I look up at the stars, there must be a million up there, "I wish I could stay here forever." I snap back to reality as I realize I said those words aloud. How childish of me. What is it with Jack? It is as if I lose any hold of my self-restraint. I slowly turn to face Jack, surely he has had enough of my outbursts and is ready to never see me again. But when our eyes meet, I swear it looks like he wants to kiss me. It does not take me but two seconds to decide that I want him to kiss me also, so I turn to fully face him. Jack quickly breaks eye contact and fidgets with something in his pockets as he takes a step back. Apparently I read this moment all wrong. How stupid of me, of course he does not want to kiss me. I have been acting like a middle school girl all night long.

"Well, umm." Jack mumbles. "Ready to head back? Didn't you say you needed to get back before your friends got home? I would hate for y'all to get in an argument or something."

"Oh yeah, of course. It is getting pretty late." I take a look at my phone to check the time and like clock work, Joz texts to let me know they are headed back to the condo.

Back at the condo, I rush around to change, making it look like I was there all night. No sooner do I pull a blanket over me on the couch and turn the T.V on, the girls waltz in. While Joz and Alice head to their rooms to change, Eden sits down next to me, glaring without saying a word.

"Hey Eden. How was dinner? I bet the gumbo was so good, I'm bummed I had to miss it."

"Oh it was good. Are you feeling any better?"

"A little bit, yeah. A relaxing night definitely helped but I'm still a bit dizzy when I stand up. Maybe a good night's sleep will do the trick."

"I'm surprised to hear your walk on the beach didn't help. I mean, you looked just fine chatting it up with that stranger from the bar."

Damn it. Joz was supposed to keep them on the other half of the beach. Hundreds of scenarios race through my head as I try to decide the best response. Each one, worse than the last. So, I decide on the truth. "Eden, I can explain-"

But she interrupts me before I can. "Don't bother. You lied to us and left us on YOUR big birthday trip. The whole reason we came was to keep you company so you didn't have to be alone, yet again! But you seem to be keeping company just fine without us. Not to mention with the guy I was flirting with Saturday night. How could you?" She stands to walk away but before she does, she turns and says "I didn't tell the other girls. You can come clean or keep lying to them. Your choice." And she walks to her room, letting the door slam behind her.

I wrap myself in the blanket and head to bed, pondering everything Eden said and wondering what to do next. She had a point, they were all there for my birthday. But then again, it is *my* birthday. I should be able to spend it however and with whomever I want!. So I unlock my phone and text Jack.

'Hey Jack! Thank you again for tonight, I had a wonderful time! What are you doing tomorrow morning? There is this market in town I would love to check out. Would you be up to joining me?'

I begin to get cozy when Joz bursts in, flipping on all the lights and giving me that 'spill the tea' look of hers. I fill her in on all the details, even the part about getting the second degree from Eden.

"She can get over it. She had like what, three Mr. Rights that night? Just give her time, I am sure tomorrow will be like nothing happened." Joz is right, Eden always overreacts and dives in, emotions first. But she always gets over things just as quickly.

Once again, I get cozy and begin to drift off to sleep when I am interrupted once more. However, this time it is not by Joz. Rather it is my own thoughts as I replay the night over again. Jack seemed to know a lot about me before I could say anything. How did he know about Shadow? Or the tent my family had growing up? Can that all really be a coincidence? I suppose it had to be. I mean, how else would he have known? He must just be extremely intuitive and can easily read people. But did he know where I was staying? I never did tell him the condo we were in but as we were walking back, Jack did seem to know where to turn without me ever saying a word. I must have begun turning and he simply followed my lead. Again, he does seem intuitive. There is no possible way he knew we were staying at the

Phoenix. I really must stop watching all those True Crime documentaries.

CHAPTER 7: THE COLORADO KILLER

Wednesday, June 17

Like a child on Christmas morning, I jump out of bed and quickly get through my morning routine. Coffee and the morning news can wait. I have a beautiful ginger in my wine cellar waiting for the grand finale. And I have exactly 2 hours to clean up before meeting Fiona at the market.

As I open the cellar door, I can tell Laine had a restless night. By the look of her swollen eyes, she spent her last night crying instead of sleeping.

"Good morning Laine. You ready to die?" I take it that by her screams she means yes. "Good. Now the only question is should we make it fast and painless or slow and exciting?"

"Ple-ase." She begs. But this time, it is as if she is begging for her death rather than her life. Just the way I like them.

"Be patient my dear. Your time is coming, I promise. Remember, you are my first in Alabama, I want to make sure you are perfect. They are going to remember you. And they will remember me even more when I sign my work." I reach for my carving knife and slowly begin to trace 'C.K' into her abdomen as she lets out piercing screams that are music to my ears. "That's it my dear, let it out. Scream away."

I take a step back to relish my craftsmanship. "You're a masterpiece Laine."

Fifteen stab wounds later, Laine takes her final breath as I breathe it in. Letting the thrill overtake me for just a moment. My final act is ripping the flower necklace off from around her neck. It will make for a perfect keepsake. I quickly clean her up and redress her, but not before tagging her wrist. In my most professional handwriting, I write *Killed: June; Hunter: The Colorado Killer,* on a small piece of paper, attach it to a piece of twine, and tie it around her wrist. And as proper, encase the tag in a small plastic bag. I will dispose of the carcass on my way to meet Fiona. And I know just the place.

After leaving Shoreline's, where I first met Laine and where Ross, the busboy, will find her body, I decide there is just enough time to take my car back home and walk to the market.

On my walk, I think back to Fiona on the pier. I should have kissed her when I had the chance. She probably thinks I am a prude. Who cares what she thinks though, it is not like she will be alive long enough for it to matter. I just have to find a way to get her back to the house and into the wine cellar.

I am dreaming about the different ways I will torture Fiona and her friends when I see her. Standing there in a beautiful white floral dress smelling flowers from one of the vendors. One second, I am picturing myself shocking her with my cattle prod as she finally sees the real me, and the next I see myself walking up behind her, spinning her around, and kissing her. What is wrong with me? I have never had any other thoughts than the one of the sweet thrill I get from torturing my victim. I brush both thoughts out of my head and settle for hollering her name as I approach.

She smiles at the sound of her name and turns towards me. "Jack! Hey, good morning!"

"You look stunning!" They are the only words I can produce on a whim. Every previous thought is stolen from my mind by her beauty.

"Well thank you!" She blushes as if she is not used to the compliments. "I was just talking to Declan here. He's telling me about his fields where he grows all these flowers."

"Hey man." I hate meeting new people. The small talk and pleasantries are exhausting. I would much rather be thinking of how I would end them versus talking about the weather that we can both obviously see for ourselves. However, I know I should pretend I am interested for Fiona's sake so I offer to buy her some flowers of her choice.

"These are so beautiful." Fiona exclaims as she breathes in their fragrance for the fifth time while we walk through the different vendors. When I respond with just a smile, she continues. "They're Tithonia Rotun-folia, I don't remember but the Mexican Sunflower. Declan was saying he only grows these because they are his sister's favorite. You will never believe what he told me!" She pauses for effect. That or for me to respond with excitement towards the coming gossip.

"What's that?" I ask with the most enthusiasm I can muster.

"Declan's sister? Apparently she's missing! Last time anyone heard from her she was meeting some friends for a drink but when she left, they never heard from her or seen her since. That was last Friday! Could you imagine? A loved one going missing? Poor guy!"

A million thoughts race through my head. I knew Fiona's flower choice looked familiar. The flower necklace I ripped from Laine's neck; it was the Mexican Sunflower. She must be Declan's sister.

Well, she was his sister. I did not think today could get any better, yet here we are. The sensation of meeting a victim's family member was more than I expected. I will have to stop by on our way out to get him to talk about her. Then I can relive her torture vicariously through his pain.

"Oh, fresh shrimp!" Fiona gasps, startling me from my thoughts. "I have the perfect recipe for this. I told the girls I would make dinner tomorrow night since I missed them last night. I just need to pick up a few more things. Do you mind stopping?"

Not bothering to answer, I bring up last night. "How was everything when you got back last night? Any trouble?"

"Oh, it was fine. They were just bummed is all."

"That's good. So what's this recipe?"

"It's a shrimp saganaki. A greek dish with shrimp cooked in a savory tomato sauce. Then you add some feta cheese." She explains as she squeezes the different cheeses. "I think I told you last night how I have always dreamed of traveling the world."

"Yeah, you were telling me you would go to Europe first."

"Well, in the meantime, since I cannot experience Europe physically, I try to experience other countries anyway I can. Specifically, by cooking traditional meals from all over the world."

"What better way to experience culture than food?" I acknowledge. I have never really cared to experience other cultures. My current way of life is enough for me. But if she is interested in it, I will play along if it means gaining her trust and getting her alone.

"Exactly!" The excitement shining through her eyes tells me I am on the right path. I cannot wait to watch that excitement turn into fear and dismay as I introduce her to my true self in my wine cellar. But then the weirdest thing happened. I felt a pang deep in my gut at the mere thought of Fiona in pain. Imagining this beautifully wild woman hurting leaves me motionless. Is this what empathy feels like? I have never endured empathy and to be honest, I never truly cared too. It would just muddy my whole way of living.

Out of nowhere, thunder begins to roll through the air and rain starts to pour down as Fiona is picking out the last of her ingredients. Fiona looks at me puzzled as we did not expect this big of a thunderstorm to come through.

"Well this came out of nowhere!" She hollers over the sound of rain hitting the tents.

Then, like a lightbulb turning on, I get the perfect idea. "I just live right around the corner. We can wait out the storm there. Want to make a run for it?"

She does not answer immediately, causing me to

wonder if I spoke too soon and ruined any chance to get her alone. "Let's do it!" She finally responds with a wild grin.

And just like that, I am on my way to capture my 16th victim. If only I can get these feelings out of the way first.

CHAPTER 8: FIONA

Wednesday, June 17

Jack opens the front door and we rush inside. We are both drenched from the sudden downpour yet I could not feel more free. I cannot remember the last time I got caught in the rain. Maybe Jack really is someone I can be my true self with. Someone I could let go of this facade, let my walls down, and finally be the real me.

"Wait here," Jack instructs. "I'll go grab us some dry clothes. I'm sure I have something that won't be too big for you."

As Jack heads down the hallway to the left, I take a moment to glance around the room to get a better idea of who Jack is. He may not say much, but someone's belongings will always tell you about their owner. For instance, from my spot in the entryway, I confirm that Jack is a simple man, not needing much other than the essentials. By the lack of photos in the living room, I assume he is not close to his family. Maybe the reason he has not mentioned them is because of a difficult separation and not that he does not want me to know about them. As I spy half carved wood blocks in the corner, Jack comes back holding a pair of sweatpants that have been cut into shorts and an old Oak Ridge Boys t-shirt. So he likes old country music, that is another thing I did not know about Jack. I have never personally listened to them before, but I remember my dad used to talk about them all the time and would play their records in his office while he worked. That is, before he left us.

Jack interrupts my memory of the dead beat who calls himself my father, "You can change in the bathroom. Down this hallway, it's the first door on the right."

Yet again Jack surprises me. Not as if I wanted him to, but most men I know would prefer you change right then and there. They would not even give you the option to change in private. Just more proof that Jack is not like any other man I know.

In the bathroom, I look around as I peel off my wet dress. A single toothbrush with a squeezed tube of toothpaste, a wadded up hand towel, and a razor all sit on the counter. Not the most organized I see.

When I walk back to the living room, Jack is starting a pot of coffee in the kitchen. "Let me just finish this up real quick and I'll throw that in the dryer for you." He says, pointing to the sopping wet dress in my hands. I attempted to wring it out in the sink but when I look down, I see it is still dripping onto the wood floor.

The second Jack steps out of eyesight with my dress, I take a closer look around his house. A small kitchen table sits in the far corner of the dining room with only two chairs. But by the look of the mail, newspapers, and random things thrown on the table, I doubt he has ever actually enjoyed a meal at it. After taking a step closer to the table to inspect the mail, I see something that vaguely resembles a scrapbook laying under a couple days worth of newspapers. The sight instantly brings me back to the night we had our terrifying encounter with an intruder. I shudder at the memory. How can anyone break into someone else's home and steal something? Let alone a personal item such as a scrapbook of all things.

Jack startles me when he walks back into the room. "Excuse the mess. I've been busy working extra hours, I haven't taken time to go through the mail."

"Oh, you're fine. I was just taking in-" I pause to quickly decide how to cover up my real thoughts. Not ready to tell him of the break-in or the rotten fish left at our doorstep. "the wood carvings. Did you make all those?"

He follows my eyes to the carvings in the living room, then the partially carved wood blocks strewn throughout the dining room. "Yeah those are all mine. It makes for a great distraction."

"That's so awesome! You're really good. Do you sell them?"

"Not really. They're more like a keepsake for me. Each time I look at one I remember exactly where I was when the idea popped into my head and allows me to relive that moment over and over again."

"Wow! That is so neat! It's like your very own journal." I carefully pick one up. "Tell me about this one." It was a carving of a mountain lion standing tall on its hind legs about to pounce.

"That one is from a hunt in Colorado last Spring." Jack closes his eyes as if the memories from the hunt come back to him.

"It must have been a pretty special hunt to make the shelf of carvings." I add, trying to get Jack to open up even more.

"It was a great hunt. Until the two I really wanted got away." Jack turns and heads back down the hallway with no further explanation as to the hunt in Colorado. But before he gets too far, he hollers over his shoulder, "Want to watch a movie?" I guess our discussion about his wood carvings and his past is over. For now at least.

"Sure, I would love that! Do you have anything in mind?"

Moments later, Jack walks back into the living room holding a small stack of DVDs. "I'll let you make the final decision. I picked out Silence of the Lambs, Jaws, Split, or Gone Girl."

"Oh, I'm usually not big on scary movies." I pause a second, hoping Jack would take the hint to choose different movies but he simply stands there holding out the stack for me to see. "But I'll give one of these a try. They can't be too bad I suppose. Let's go with Jaws this time." I have never seen it but I figure it is a good thriller to dip my toes into. No pun intended.

As Jack starts the movie, I make my way to the couch and get cozy with the blanket.

"I almost forgot, do you want some coffee?"

"That sounds great! But do you have any creamer by chance?" No matter how many times I have tried to be sophisticated and drink black coffee, I cannot drink more than one sip.

"No, but I can doctor it up for you if you'd like. Do you prefer caramel or chocolate?"

"How about both?" This will be interesting I think to myself.

Moments later, Jack comes back holding two cups of coffee. I inspect the contents, inhaling the rich aroma and then carefully lift the cup to my lips and take a sip.

As soon as the steaming liquid hits my tastebuds, I cannot get it down fast enough before I exclaim, "Wow, this is really good!"

"You seem surprised."

"It's just that it tastes like something I would get from the coffee shop. I've never been able to recreate something like this at home before."

"Well, being a bartender isn't too far from a barista. You're still mixing different flavors to create a whole new delicacy."

Letting out a laugh, "You can be my barista any day!" When he looks back at me, I swear I see a hint of bashfulness in his eyes. But rather than responding, he nuzzles back into the couch inches from me and pushes play.

After the movie is over, I sit here for a moment to collect my thoughts. "That wasn't so bad! I actually kind of enjoyed it!" I pause then add, "It may be a little bit before I go swimming in the ocean again but still." I laugh, this time Jack joins in with a single laugh. Which is the most I have gotten from him since first meeting him two days ago.

"That one's a classic around these parts. I probably don't go a single day without someone making a joke or reference to that movie."

"Really? I can honestly say, I don't think I've ever

heard someone make a reference from that one."

"That you know of. Maybe now that you've seen it, you may pick up on more references." I am taken aback by the harshness of his response but before I can dwell on it too long, he asks, "Are you hungry at all?"

"Oh, umm, yeah." Jack does not have a filter and will transition conversations with no warning, leaving me constantly guessing what he will say next. "I could eat a little something. I'm not too terribly hungry though."

"Alright, let me check and see what I have." After a few moments rummaging through cabinets and the refrigerator, Jack hollers, "I have an unopened jar of cheese dip that I can zap in the microwave real quick."

"Yeah! That actually sounds phenomenal right now!" I already planned to say yes to whatever Jack suggested, not wanting to be a hassle, but chips and hot cheese actually would be great right now.

"How about a game of chess?" Jack asks as he walks back into the living room and places a bag of chips and the bowl of cheese on the coffee table.

"Oh, umm-" so much for me not being a hassle. "I actually don't know how to play chess. I've always wanted to learn but it hasn't clicked for me."

"No problem, it's tough for a lot of people. I got a new

puzzle, want to try your hand at that?"

"Now that I can do! I love puzzles, something about them is so peaceful."

"Perfect. Wait here, I'll go get it. Help yourself to some cheese."

It is not until I take that first bite of a chip that I realize I am more hungry than I originally thought. I will have to be sure to distract myself with this puzzle so I do not eat too much and come off like a pig. Mom always said to watch how much you eat on a date and I already made a fool of myself at dinner last night.

"Here's a good one." Jack says as he sits down on the floor across from me. I pick up the box to get a closer look as he clears newspaper and books from the coffee table to make room for the puzzle. 1,000 pieces for a beautiful rustic cabin set back in the woods.

"This one will be beautiful." I remark. "Tough with all the dark color tones but that's what makes them fun to put together."

Over the next two hours, Jack and I work relentlessly on the puzzle. Once again, the conversation comes easily, especially having a puzzle to focus on instead of contemplating every word before I speak. As we are nearing the end of the puzzle, the pile of pieces becomes less and less. Making it easier to *accidentally* brush my hand against his. The first time he pulled his hand back in shock and quickly apologized. But now, even he is grazing his pinky against mine. I cannot help but wonder if he is feeling the same sensation I am when our hands touch. I try to watch his eyes to gain some idea of what he is thinking but he continues to remain a mystery.

Jack lets me put in the final piece and we both sit back to take in our masterpiece as he tells me, "It reminds me of this cabin I visited back in Colorado. I could spend hours there."

"I'm sure it was beautiful. I've never been to the mountains. I've actually never considered it. When planning vacations, I just pick the beach or another big city."

"Are you serious? You should go at least once. Just to experience the stillness. I'm telling you, the mountains are something else."

"Well then, maybe I will just have to start planning my next vacation. Want to help me? Tell me all the must-see stops?" I hold his gaze longer than usual, trying to communicate more with my eyes than my words.

"Yeah, I can do that." He stated matter of factly. "Ready for a second movie?" It was not the response I hoped for. This man is probably the hardest person to read that I have ever met. One moment I think he yearns to kiss me and the next, like I am a stranger to him.

"Of course. Your turn to pick."

Jack jumps up and starts a new movie without another word. But, when he sits back down next to me, he closes the gap between us and stretches his arm behind my neck. As the opening credits begin to roll, I realize I am not ready for the film he chose. Between the creepy music and the brief flashes of a woman being wheeled down a long corridor with only half the lights working, I can already tell this will not be an enjoyable movie. I do not know who could find a movie about a serial killer with multiple personalities actually relaxing but here we are, watching Split at 4:00 o'clock in the afternoon like it is any other movie.

With every change of personality, I lean in closer to Jack. And by the time the Beast appears and kills Karen, I jump and immediately grab for his arm while I bury my head into his shoulder waiting for it to be over. When I look back up, embarrassed at what Jack must think of me, I see a hint of amusement mixed with what I can only describe as strained sympathy. I swallow my ego, lean in, not losing his gaze, and kiss him. To my surprise, Jack did not pull away. Like a magnet, I use my lips as an anchor and pull him even closer to me. At that moment, Jack takes the lead and gently lowers me back on the couch. His hand finds its way around my waist as he toys with the hemline of my shirt.

Taking my lack of hesitation as a cue, Jack slides his hand up my shirt and fondles my breast. Although my body instantly responds to the sensation, my mind does not. My breathing is getting deeper and my back arches as my body screams for more. But my mind cannot help but focus on him, or the lack thereof. That is until he pulls the shirt over my head and unsnaps my bra, exposing my breasts to the cool air. He leans down, kissing and nibbling each one while his hands travel back to my waistline. By the time he has the sweatpants off of me, I am only thinking about one thing; how I want him.

Like any other man I have slept with, Jack is not one to cuddle afterwards. He interrupts the silent ecstasy, "That was great. I don't know about you, but I worked up an appetite." And there goes any romance that was hanging in the air.

"Umm- yeah, I could go for some dinner." I tried all I could from not showing the disappointment that I felt. I mean, he was right. The sex was amazing and I was hungry. That cheese dip did not last very long. But I cannot help that a part of me still longs for a man with a romantic side. "I bought all that stuff for Shrimp Saganaki. Are you up to trying some Greek food?"

"I thought that was for tomorrow night?"

"I can always whip something else together for tomorrow. I would rather share this with you. All I need is full access to the kitchen. Oh, and your spice cabinet."

"It's all yours." He says, gesturing his arm towards the kitchen. "Just tell me what you need me to do."

I stand up, pulling my thong on with me. I slip back into Jack's sweatpants, fasten my bra and make my way to the kitchen, leaving the borrowed shirt lying on the living room floor. As I stir in garlic to the sauteed onion, Jack slips up behind me, placing one hand on my lower back as he slowly glides it around to my stomach. I know I made the right decision to cook in just my bra and sweatpants as he pushes his full body against my back. We move rather rhythmically, with Jack cutting and dicing and me over the stove stirring everything to perfection. So maybe I was wrong about Jack not being romantic, because I would say this is the most romantic moment I have ever shared with someone.

"What do you say after we clean this up we head to Shoreline's for a drink? Your dress should be dry by now." We are sitting on the living room floor eating at the coffee table. It was easier to move the puzzle instead of all the newspaper and items gathered on the kitchen table. Which I do not mind, it is just another reason Jack is not like the rest.

"An Amaretto Sour would be wonderful! And Shoreline's is one I haven't been to yet."

As we walk up to Shoreline's front patio, I first notice the silence. When I look around, I see there is no one else around and all the lights are off. "Where is everyone? Are they even open?" Then I notice the police tape.

"Oh, don't worry. I know another way in." Jack says as he leads me around to the side, completely ignoring the crime scene, and begins to fidget with a window.

"I don't know Jack. We shouldn't be here." I say as I look again at the crime tape blocking off the back porch.

"Come on, don't tell me you've never snuck in some place. Not even at a movie theater?"

"Well," I stop, too ashamed to tell the truth that I have never broken the law. Not even a speeding ticket, let alone break into a crime scene.

Thankfully, Jack speaks up and saves me from having to admit my embarrassing truth. "If it helps, I work here. So is it really breaking in if I'm an employee?"

I do not answer, unsure of what to say. My gut is still screaming it is wrong but my heart recalls the toe-curling sex we had 2-hours ago and yearns for round two. So I watch as Jack shimmies through the now open window and I walk back around the corner to meet him at the patio door.

Once inside, Jack leads me to the bar where he begins to make us drinks. But what he is mixing into my drink does not go into an Amaretto Sour. Although I am skeptical when he hands me the glass, I decide it is best not to question him, he is a bartender after all. I cautiously take a sip; "Oh my! This is delicious!"

"I'm glad you like it. I've been trying to get the boss to put it on my menu ever since I got here. But she's not the most open to new ideas."

"She's missing out! I mean, I would never have thought mixing bourbon into a cocktail would be good, but this is incredible! What would you call it? How about the Bama Moon?"

"Oh, that's cute." He smiles. "I was thinking more along the lines of Killer Sunrise."

"Yeah, that is way better. I would go with that one." I give an embarrassed laugh "I never was the creative one. You should keep trying to add it to the menu though, plenty of people would buy it."

"I have thought about doing something about it." Jack trails off as if daydreaming about how to get his boss to give him a shot. "We'll see what happens." Was all he added before walking towards the patio doors. I take that as my cue to follow him.

"So what is with the crime tape everywhere?" I finally ask, unable to hold my curiosity any longer.

"Oh that." I begin to think that is all he was going to say about the situation but he continues as he walks through the door. "The busboy found a girl back there this morning. Her uh- her body was thrown out with the morning trash."

WHAT? "Wait. Did you just say a body was found? Why is no one talking about this?" If it were not for the police tape and markers on the porch, I would not believe him. How is he not more concerned about the fact that a killer is out there? Like this thing happens all the time around here.

"Yeah, it's pretty crazy." He says, his back still towards me as he reaches the fire pit. Instead of taking a seat on the cushioned bench, Jack pulls the blanket off the back and spreads it over the deck next to the fire pit. I take the hint that he does not wish to talk about the girl any longer and drop my incessant questioning. It is a mood killer and I am just getting used to the romantic Jack that has shown himself.

While he begins to start the fire, I grab the pillows off the bench and make myself comfortable on the blanket. As if reading my mind about craving him again, Jack lies down next to me and instead of speaking, he kisses me softly as his hands find their way under my dress. This time there is something different about him. Whereas before in the living room, it was as though his body was going through the motions but Jack was not there. The intimate connection that often comes with sex was missing.

But not this time. This time I feel the connection drawing me in. I wrap my arms around him and slide one hand down his pants, squeezing his firm butt. I dig my other hand into his shoulder blade, pulling him tighter into me. He is gentle as he caresses my hip with one hand and holds my neck in the other. He tenderly tugs at my thong before sliding his hand to my breast and tracing my bra line with his fingers, teasing me to my breaking point.

"Roll over." I demand in a breathless voice as I push him to his back and swing my leg over to straddle him. I remove Jack's shirt and lean down to kiss him, leaving a trail of kisses from his lips to his happy trail just above his pant line. I pause to meet Jack's gaze, his eyes demanding me to keep going. I leave him wanting more just a moment longer as I pull my dress off and unsnap my bra. I seductively hold it out with my finger, letting it slide slowly off while Jack takes in my body, for what seems to be the first time. Just before I feel like he has reached his edge, I yank his pants down, exposing his erect boner, and mount him. Taking full control, I begin slow and seductive, letting my hands explore his body while he explores mine. Once my body feels the rhythm, slowly forward, with a forceful thrust in, I can no longer hold on and lose my restraint. I ride him faster and harder as our moans fill the night air. Until finally our bodies give in to the sensation and I collapse on top of him in one final moan.

Once we catch our breath, I roll over and rest my

head on his chest, not letting him get away from a bit of cuddling this time. "I had a really great time with you today." I whisper.

"You know, I think this is the most fun I have had in a long time. Which is weird for me."

"How's that?" I ask confused.

"Oh um-" he took a nervous breath in before continuing, "I just didn't think I could have fun with another person like this is all. What was your favorite part of today?"

I pretend to think about it although I know right away my favorite part. Rather parts. "Let's see. The market was a lot of fun. Then getting caught in the rain and getting to cook a new meal." I look at him before letting out a laugh, "I'm kidding!" It was cute how Jack seemed disappointed in my answer. "My true favorite part was getting to put the puzzle together with you and listening to your stories. And then there's all the sensational sex we had." With that last tidbit, Jack's lips curled slightly as he tried to hide his enjoyment.

"That has been pretty great hasn't it? So great, there could even be round three?" He asks as he rolls over on top of me and fucks me even harder and deeper than before.

Once we finish, we lay back to catch our breath. And just like that, the sex guru is gone and rather than the romantic Jack taking its place, the absent one returns. A hundred thoughts run through my head as Jack stands and pulls on his shorts. *'Did I do something wrong? Did I not praise him when he did that move? Is he tired of being with me?'* I decide no matter what it is, there is only one response.

"I should probably head back to the condo. The girls might be getting worried why I haven't come back yet." Too embarrassed to stand up naked, I pull my dress over my head while still sitting.

"I understand, I'll walk you back. You shouldn't be alone when there's a killer out there."

CHAPTER 9: THE COLORADO KILLER

Thursday, June 18

On the porch, I sip my coffee and listen to the ocean waves hit the shore. The storm yesterday has gone but strong winds remain, causing fierce waves. I am more of a mountain man myself but I respect the power of the ocean. The way it can subdue anything and anyone. With each crash of the waves, I lose myself in my thoughts of Fiona more and more. Yesterday was the most fun I have had in a long time. Not the kind of fun that killing brings, this was a feeling that I have not felt in years. I cannot help but think the amount of enjoyment torturing Fiona will bring. To watch the betrayal fill her eyes as any hope dissipates. I want to kill Fiona. But I also wish I wanted to kill her enough to actually go through with it. There is something about her that I cannot take myself to hurt her. I had every opportunity yesterday yet rather than locking her up, I kissed her. Just thinking about her sensual touch on my body sends me to the edge. I have not felt this way about a woman in four years. Since Rebecca; the one who made me The Colorado Killer.

I used to only break into rich folks homes and take what I wanted. All my life people took from me, it was time I started taking for myself. That was, until I saw Rebecca again, walking home holding hands with Liam. About a year before that night, I was at the bar with Rebecca. I had a crush on her for months and finally got the nerve up to ask her out for drinks. We were not there but 30 minutes when Liam walked in and began flirting with her. When I walked Rebecca back to her place, she made up some lame excuse, saying she had a great time but was too busy with school for a relationship. Must not have been that busy because a week later, I saw her having drinks with Liam.

When I saw them together that hot summer night and watched as Liam followed her inside, I lost all restraint. This feeling that I did not know I had been suppressing deep inside broke loose. I stayed outside her house watching. I watched the front door open as Liam stepped outside. I watched as Rebecca stood on her tip toes and kissed him goodbye. I watched as Liam walked down the street and the lights inside shut off. That is when I made my move. I was not sure what I was going to do, I just knew I had to do it. I gave the front door knob a jiggle as I simultaneously nudged the door with my elbow, causing the door to open without a sound. A lot of those old houses have weak locks. Just have to hold it the right way and they break loose. Good for me, but bad for the homeowners. One would assume they would use their money to secure their possessions but I suppose they think their wealth makes them untouchable.

Once inside Rebecca's home, I hid myself in the shadows and watched as she prepared for bed. I began to feel the rush of adrenaline consume me while she washed her face. It was better than simply stealing when no one was home. After she checked all the doors and windows to ensure they were locked, I knew that was my cue. I grabbed the object closest to me, a kitchen knife, and stepped out of the shadows to reveal myself. I felt another surge of rage strengthen me when she did not recognize my face. But the look of terror in her eyes was priceless. Just remembering it brings me that same high as it did that night. I knew then that I could not stop. I had to have it again and again.

But not with Fiona. She is different, special. When she looks at me, she sees me. Not like Rebecca, or Ryan, or Laine or all the others I have killed. They all thought they were better than me, turning up their nose when they walked by. Fiona on the other hand actually listens and cares about what I have to say. So unless she gives me a reason, I do not think I can bring myself to hurt her.

Picking up my phone, I decide to text her. *'Good morning beautiful.'* Wait, no, that is too forward. *'Good morning. I can't stop thinking about yesterday and seeing you in the fire light.'* That sounds good right? Leave the next move to her if she wants to see me again. "Screw it." I say aloud and click send. I do not have the energy to worry over a simple text. Within seconds my phone dings to the sound of an incoming text message. She says how much she enjoyed yesterday but makes no mention of another date. So, I choose to go ahead and ask her myself. But when she texts back again, she says no. With a lame excuse that she has to stay back with her friends today. As the rage of rejection begins to boil up, Fiona texts again.

'I'm really sorry! When I got back last night all the girls were super mad that I ditched them on our girls getaway so to make up for it, I promised them I'd hang out with them today. But I can get away tomorrow! I would love to see you again before I left!'

She is lucky. Her last text diffused the bomb building up inside me and saved me from killing her afterall. But like any drug, I felt the craving for a kill and I must feed it. So I get cleaned up and head into town to find my new victim number 16.

Walking through town, I wait for the perfect prey. I cannot just take anyone. It must be someone who walks through life believing they are untouchable.

That their status or possessions will save them from harm. Only then will I get to see the true fear as any pride and hope is pushed out by hopelessness.

And the hunt is on. A beautiful brunette struts past me, her oversized beach bags shoving me as she passes.

"Hey, watch it lady." I huff. The pretentious bitch turns around solely so she can raise her nose higher and swing her hips even more. Her mistake. I follow her through the streets and the various high-end shops. Watch as she tries on the latest swimsuits, settling for the yellow bikini. I myself think she should have gone with the red one but she will not be alive long enough to wear either one. After enjoying her shopping spree, she stops by The Shack, a food truck known for its chili cheese fries. I slip in line right behind her. Targets like this one do not require much stealth, they are entirely oblivious to anything or anyone outside their bubble.

I cannot help but chuckle when she orders the chili cheese fries without the chili. "You're missing out." I speak up.

She quickly snaps her head in direction. "Excuse me?"

"I said you're missing out. Bruce here makes the best chili in Orange Beach."

"Well, I'm vegetarian." She snarks, looking me up and down as if I am a monster for eating meat. She will soon know the kind of monster I can be. Once we both finish our fries, mine with extra chili just for her, I continue my hunt by stalking my prey and learning her habits. Until I find my perfect shot. I know she is too heartless to lure with a call for help so I go with the good 'ol grab from behind technique. When we find ourselves in the parking lot, I quietly sneak up behind her.

"Hello again. Remember me?" I startle her.

"Umm, no." It was all she said before giving a huff and turning back towards her car as she loads her bags into the back seat.

"Maybe next time you should learn to be more polite to people. Well, that is if you had a next time."

"Listen, I don't know-" is all she gets out before I pinch her carotid artery and she collapses in my arms. I shove her remaining bags into her back seat, slam the door, and then carry her to my car as if she is drunkenly sleeping in my arms.

The first thing my latest catch notices when she begins to awaken is the rope tying her wrists to a floor joist in my wine cellar. Then she notices me. Within seconds, she is pulling at the rope, wiggling her whole body, and screaming. "Who are you? Where am I? What do you want?"

My favorite part. The first glimpse of hopelessness

yet still enough hope to think they will somehow survive. "Of course, where are my manners? My name is Jack. But you may know me better as The Colorado Killer." She instantly screams in response. "Ahh, so you have heard of me?" I let her cry and scream until she tires herself before I continue. "First thing you should know, you can scream as loud as you want. I promise you, no one will hear you. No one will find you. I have been doing this for 4 years. You are my 16th precious prize. Understand?" I take her somber sobs as confirmation. "So, I told you my name. What's yours?" I slam my hand down on the metal counter next to me when she does not answer and scream, "What is your name?"

"B- Br- Brook- Brooklyn."

"Brooklyn? See, that was not so hard was it?" I ask, composing myself before continuing. "Second thing you should know, Brooklyn, is this is your fault. I don't just hunt innocent people you know." Picking up a knife, I slowly walk towards her, letting terror set in more and more with each step. "We're going to take things nice and slow now." I inform her as I begin cutting her clothes off piece by piece.

Once Brooklyn is fully naked, I step back and take in my full prize. Even through the tears silently rolling down her face, she is beautiful. Not like Fiona level beautiful but not terrible on the eyes either. "Well Brooklyn, I think this is enough for now. Why don't you get comfortable for the evening?"

Back upstairs in the living room, I note the time. 7 o'clock in the evening. After this morning's text, I have not heard from Fiona and cannot help but think about how her evening is going. I may be new to relationships but I know enough to not text her on girls' night when we have only seen each other a handful of times. So I will do one better, I will go over to her condo and check in on her.

Once I reach her condo, I immediately spot her patio. Second floor, third from the right. The same one I watched her walk into Monday night. The same patio trellis I climbed up when I broke in and took the scrapbook. I notice all the lights are off except one stand alone lamp in the living room, so I take my chance and climb up to her patio to get a better view.

I see four girls all huddled together; two on the couch and two on a blanket fort in front of the couch. I cannot tell what movie they are watching but from the way their lips curl up and the muffled sound of laughter through the glass, I take it they are watching some comedy. Fiona looks absolutely stunning when she laughs. And there she goes, sending another jab to my gut by having such a great time without me. I know I should be happy for her to have these friends in her life, but I cannot help but wonder if she is going to run back to Kansas City and forget about the phenomenal night we had yesterday. The only thing I can think to do now is have a little fun while I can.

I silently climb down the trellis and make a run to the market. Strategizing my next moves carefully. Luckily for me, I am back before the movie ends. I lean close to their front door and hear the roar of laughter from inside. That is my cue.

I set my first trap there at the front door. They did not seem to appreciate the first fish I left for them so I picked a better, larger fish for their welcome mat. This time, from the market's dumpster. It will be sure to get their attention now. I scribbled a note on a napkin from one of the market's stores that read, *'You have made it this long. But don't take the night for granted.'* But I do not knock just quite yet, I want to set all my traps before I let the fun begin.

I pull out my knife and cut open the second fish I found. I dip two fingers into the belly until they are well coated in blood and write on the front door. Gathering up my mess, I take a deep breath in, inhaling the foul stench of old fish. Satisfied with my work, I give a quick bang on the door and take off for the back patio. I have another ploy but I also want to get front row seats to the show.

I make it back to the patio just in time to see the short blonde one from the bar answer the door. Her immediate squeal draws the other three to inspect the mysterious disruption to their ladies night. This ruse is playing out better than I could have hoped for as I watch their reactions. When they all examine my masterpiece, their screams say it all. Music to my ears. Unfortunately, I cannot watch from here for too long. Once they see my note on the door, they are sure to come this way. I dip my fingers back into the fish and leave a second blood drawn note on the patio door. Jumping the last two feet off the trellis, I make it to the shadows just in time for Fiona's sister to flip on the patio light as the girls erupt in more screams.

CHAPTER 10: FIONA

Thursday, June 18

It is nice to have an entire day of staying in my pajamas with the girls. Just the four of us, HBO, and all the snacks we could want. A complete girls movie day. But I also find myself thinking of Jack, of what he is up to today. I enjoyed spending a rainy day with him just as much as I am today with the girls. I felt awful sending the text this morning to tell him I cannot see him today. But after coming home late last night, I knew I needed to be with the girls today.

I expected Eden to throw a fit because it is me with the date and not her. But when Alice was the one to approach me, it was a different story. Of course her main argument was how I should treat my body as a treasure and not let just any guy off the street touch me. She then threw it in my face that she would have stayed home with Aaron and baby Iris if I was going to be off with some guy the whole time. A little exaggeration if you ask me but she has a point. The only reason they are here is to celebrate my birthday. So as much as it pained me, I told Jack I would try to see him tomorrow.

As we sit there watching Daddy's Home, it reminds me of the old days right after college when Eden and Alice would come over almost every Sunday afternoon. My mind flashes back and forth from movie nights in college and watching movies with Jack yesterday. Until a flicker of a shadow moving across the back patio door catches my eye. I stare, straining to see if I can make out a figure but when I do not see anything, I give up, thinking it was probably just a bird flying past or simply my imagination.

But when Eden's phone dings, I think maybe my first thought was right afterall.

"Guys." Eden says breathlessly. "Guys, pause the movie. I just got a text."

"So what Eden? You have guys texting you all the time." Jozlynn cannot quite hide the annoyance in her response.

"No, Joz. It's not that this time. I just got a text from a strange number"

"What does it say?" Alice asks.

"That's just it. It doesn't say anything. It's just a

picture of me from the other day when I went down to the market to grab stuff to make Shrimp Fettuccine. The picture is me talking to the seafood guy." She holds up her phone and shows us.

"Maybe it's some guy you hooked up with once and he is trying to get back at you for not calling him back." Alice says plainly. "I told you that ghosting all those guys would come back to bite you."

"That's not possible, Alice. I don't give my real number to any guy who I don't plan to see again. And I don't plan to see many of them again, so."

Before we can say anymore about the strange text message, someone knocks at our door, causing us all to jump. Alice even lets out a small yelp. Eden is the only one brave enough to answer the strange knock at this late hour. Although it is probably her irritation that drives her. She stands and confidently walks towards the door, fully prepared to lay into whoever is messing with us. But when she opens the door, I cannot see anyone standing there.

"Umm. Guys! You may want to see this!" She yells back at us without looking away at whatever was left at our door.

"Oh my gosh! Not again!" Jozlynn cries out when she reaches the door.

Eden picks up the note from the rotten fish and reads it aloud. "You have made it this long. But don't take the night for granted. What is that supposed to mean?"

"It may have something to do with this." Alice says, pointing at the blood drawn note on the door. "I'm watching you!" Now I am scared. The fish on Tuesday was weird and gross, but now a blood drawn note on our door and a photo of Eden? Someone is stalking her and we are all in the middle of it. Just then, we all get a text from the same number as Eden's stalker. But this time, it is not just a photo of Eden. It is one with all of us sitting in the living room just moments before.

"The patio!" Alice shouts. "This photo was taken from there." We all run to the sliding glass door as Jozlynn flips on the light. Simultaneously, we all let out a scream. Right there on the glass, another note written in blood. *'Missed me -CK'* My head is spinning. We all stand there, silent now, not sure what to say. Then Alice, in a hushed tone, asks, "Wh-who is CK?"

"That's it!" I say, echoing in the silence of the room.

"What is? FiFi, are you okay?" Joz asks.

"Who is CK? It was on the front page of the newspaper today. I saw it when we went out for snacks this morning. Here, I'll show you." I pull out my phone and search today's headlining story. But my excitement of connecting the clues quickly turns into despair as I read the full news article. The body they found behind Shoreline's Wednesday morning had '*C.K.*' carved into her body and a hunters tag tied around her wrist. The rush of memories hit me like an ocean wave. I stagger back until I reach the couch and lower myself to sit. The girl's voices are barely audible as they try to talk to me.

"Fifi? What's wrong, you're scaring me." Joz asks.

"More like scaring all of us. Fiona! What is it? What did you find?" Eden reaches for my phone to read it for herself. "They found a woman's body yesterday morning that had CK carved on her torso. How is this connected to us?"

"The Colorado Killer." I manage to say.

"Are we supposed to know who that is?" Alice asks, seeming to get annoyed at the lack of answers.

I take a slow, deep breath in, attempting to slow down my pounding heart, and tell them everything I know about the Colorado Killer. Although it is not much. Mainly that he has killed 14, now 15, people that we know of, that he is the reason Charlotte is in a coma back in Kansas City, and how no one knows what happened to him. Until now I suppose. Out of all the places he could have run off to hide, how did we happen to come to the same city at the same time?

"How does this have anything to do with us? If anything, he is after you. I mean you're Charlotte's friend. You have the most connection to him." Eden accuses.

Thankfully Joz steps in as I am still in shock to answer her. "Well hang on Eden. He sent you the first text which was a picture of just you. So if he is targeting anyone specific, why would it not be you? Maybe you pissed off the wrong guy." Joz and Eden spend the next few minutes arguing back and forth about whose fault it is that we are on a killer's radar.

"Never mind whose fault it is." Alice was always the first one to break up an argument with her peacemaker attitude. "What we should be talking about is what are we going to do about it? We cannot just leave this alone. Yeah, the one fish on Tuesday maybe, but this? We can't just sit here and do nothing. I mean, if this Colorado Killer is really taunting us, the authorities should know about it."

"I have to call Charlotte." I interject as I grab my phone from Eden. She will know what to do about him.

"Didn't you say she's in a coma?" Eden asks but I am already in the kitchen dialing Charlotte's number.

"Hello, Charlotte's phone." A rough voice answers.

"Umm, hello? Who is this? Mr. Hearon?"

"No, this is Liam. Charlotte's father isn't here today."

Liam? Who is Liam? "Oh, hey Liam." I say as I remember the lumberjack of a man I met at the hospital when I visited Charlotte. "This is Fiona,

Charlotte's fr- umm, co-worker" Friend may still be too strong of a word to consider us. Charlotte never did forgive me before getting attacked by the Colorado Killer.

"Fiona? The one who stabbed her in the back seven weeks before her wedding?"

I can tell this is not going to be as pleasant a conversation as I had anticipated. "Yeah, that one." I admit.

"So what is it you need?"

"I have a problem and I was hoping Charlotte could help if she was awake. It's kind of life or death."

"Well Charlotte is still in a coma. You would know that if you were a real friend and actually visited her more often." He huffed. The reality of his comment does not lessen the blow but before I can respond with some lame excuse of why I have not visited more, I hear Liam take a deep sigh on the other end of the line. "You said it's life or death?"

"Yeah, I think it might be."

"What is it?" Is all he asked but I am not about to turn away advice from someone who has seen the killer for themselves just because of his attitude. So I tell him about the Sunday night break-in, the dead fish on Tuesday, the strange text messages, and tonight's frightening encounter.

"Sounds like you have a stalker on your hands who is trying to mess with four girls on vacation. What's the life or death part?"

"The stalker? I believe it's the Colorado Killer." There was only silence coming through the receiver. "Liam? Are you still there? Did you hear what I said?"

"Yeah, sorry. What makes you think he's there?" So I tell him about the woman they found behind the bar and how tonight's note was signed C.K.

"Fiona, you have to get out of there. Right now. Who is all there with you?" I can hear his tone change as he begins taking me seriously. I would even say there is a hint of fear in his response.

"There's four of us. Where are we supposed to go? It's getting dark out and he was watching us from our patio. He could still be outside waiting for us. Can't we just call the police and tell them what I know?"

"The Orange Beach police won't do anything. Don't call them. Just lock every door, window, any possible entrance into the condo. And close all the blinds. Grab whatever weapon you can find; a kitchen knife, fireplace poker, baseball bat. But whatever you do-" Liam is interrupted by a multitude of voices shouting codes and words I cannot make out through the phone. Liam must have dropped the phone though, because I can barely make out his next words. "Charlotte! Is she okay? What is happening?" More inaudible voices in the background. "Someone tell me what is happening damn it." And the line goes dead as Liam hangs up the phone.

CHAPTER 11: THE COLORADO KILLER

Friday, June 19

Being in the good mood that I am this morning, I decide to go easy on Brooklyn. The fun from last night still has me on a high. As I am telling her about my night, I feel the surge of adrenaline flow through my veins.

"You should have seen their faces when they opened the door and saw my gift." I tell her. "I only wish I could have stayed and watched as they found my second note on the patio. But I did hear their screams from the shadows." Brooklyn lets out a whimper. Although I am not sure if it is my story that has all worked up or the knife that I am gliding up her legs, across her torso, and around her breasts. I make a small knick on her upper chest to send a hint of pain through her body. As I prepare to make a similar cut on her other side, I hear my phone buzz.

I contemplate for just a moment whether answering is important enough to interrupt my time with Brooklyn. But it might be Fiona and she will always be important enough. When I pick it up, I see a missed call from her while simultaneously receiving a text.

'Hey! I tried calling but you must be busy. I was wondering if you would be up for grabbing some brunch this morning? You will not believe the night I had!'

Without hesitating, I reply, telling her how I would love to see her this morning. "Brooklyn, my dear. Are you okay to stay here? Does only having one cut bother you? I can always give you another quick knick before I go." I cannot help but smile when she cries out *'No'*.

Fiona can barely get through the pleasantries and ordering her food before jumping in and telling me every bit of last night. With each detail she speaks, I relive it in my mind, feeling the high come back to me. The blood drawn notes were especially a hit. I am glad I decided to pick up that second fish when I saw it laying there. The entire conversation was going great and paired nicely with my steak and eggs, until she mentioned the last part.

"You called who?" I asked, not thinking I heard her correctly.

"My friend Charlotte. Well I called her phone but

ended up talking to her boyfriend, Liam because my friend is in a coma." Ahh, so they were alive.

"Oh, what did he have to say?"

"Well, I'm not exactly sure. He started telling me what we should do. He said not to call the cops but then something happened to Charlotte and he hung up without finishing his advice."

"I see." My mind is spinning with thoughts. Excitement that Charlotte might die after all. Exhilaration that Liam is watching the love of his life slowly slip away from him instead of a quick stab to the heart. But distraught at the thought of what he might do knowing I was here. "Well I hope your friend is okay. But he is right about not calling the cops."

"What? How is not calling the police a good thing?"

"I just mean none of you were hurt. You don't know for sure if this so-called Colorado Killer is after you. It could be some punk teenagers who read the paper and want to mess with four girls on vacation."

"I suppose you have a point. So far it has all been harmless pranks to scare us." She says, sulking back into her chair as if a weight has been lifted.

Thankfully I diffused her wanting to call the police but I feel a slight twinge at the thought that Fiona was as scared as she was last night. But between the high drowning out any emotion and seeing her relief just now, I bask once more in the memories of last night.

As the waitress takes our plates, I know our time together is coming to an end and I have to ask her something I never thought I would ask another woman. "So when are y'all leaving Alabama?" Not the question I wanted to ask but it is at least in the right direction.

"We're actually leaving tomorrow. We have to be at the airport at 2 o'clock tomorrow afternoon."

"Wow. So soon already? Didn't y'all just get into town?"

"Feels that way." She laughs. "But we got in late Saturday night."

"Stay." I blurt out before I can stop myself.

"What?" Her confused eyes look back at me.

"I'm sorry. What I meant to say was, would you stay? Here. With me. We don't even have to stay in Orange Beach. We could go wherever you want to go. You name it, Paris, Texas, Maine, Greece. Say the word and we can go." I stop myself too late. I was babbling like a fool. Here is this beautiful woman that I only met five days ago. She would be crazy if she uprooted her life for a complete stranger.

"Jack." Of course, only the best rejections start off with your name. "I would absolutely love that." Wait a minute, did she really just say what I think she said? "I have really enjoyed the few days we have spent together." She pauses. "But I don't know. My life is back in Kansas City. My family, friends, my job."

"Yeah, no. I get it. I shouldn't have asked."

"Can I think about it?"

I smile, too dumbfounded to actually respond. Is she really considering staying with me? Or is she simply saying that to ease the rejection?

As I watch Fiona walk down the street towards her condo, I wonder if this will be the last time I see her. Maybe I will meet her at the airport tomorrow and put an end to her once and for all. Then she will have to stay with me forever.

When I return home, my mind is plagued with thoughts of Fiona. Going back and forth whether I should let her live or kill her. Sitting makes the thoughts worse so I take my frustration and indecisiveness out on Brooklyn. Slicing her chest, ripping out her toe nails, even cutting one of them off. I keep going, oblivious to her screams, until I tire too much to continue. Looking into Brooklyn's eyes, I know she does not have much fight left in her but I also know that she is not ready.

"Okay, my dear. I think you have had enough for today. I will leave you to rest." I turn off the lights, shut the basement cellar door behind me, and trudge upstairs to the bedroom.

In the shower, my thoughts once again go to Fiona. But this time, I am not asking myself what if she does not stay, rather what if she does? I know if Fiona stays then my extracurricular hunting would have to be hidden better if not come to an end all together. Could I really put an end to The Colorado Killer though? That is my legacy.

CHAPTER 12: FIONA

Saturday, June 20

"Joz!" I holler from my room. Today is my birthday and the day our girls' vacation comes to an end. We are all spending the morning packing before we have to head to the airport. But I am spending more time going over the pros and cons list in my head than packing. In just a few more hours, I need to decide whether or not I will get on that airplane, leaving Jack behind for good. We decided last night we would go to the beach one last time for a nice birthday lunch so I still have some time to make my decision. But either way, we need to have our stuff out of the condo before we leave for lunch.

"What's up?" Joz asks as she plops down on my bed, not bothering to move my folded piles of clothes out of the way.

"I don't know." Is all I can say as I fall back onto the

other half of my clothes on the bed.

"What do you mean? Did you just call me in here so I can watch you not pack?"

"No." I whine. "You know how I went to brunch yesterday with Jack?"

"Yeah."

"Well, I didn't tell you everything." I pause to take a breath. "Jack asked me to stay."

"Like stay another day?"

"No, like stay. Move away somewhere with him."
"What?" She shrieked. "What did you tell him? Obviously you told him no but like how? What did he do?"

"I actually asked him if I could think about it."

"Fiona. What? You don't even know this guy. Why are you even considering it?"

"I don't know. Think about it Joz. What do I have waiting for me in Kansas City? I cannot go back to work without Char being there. You should have heard Liam on the phone Thursday night. I don't know if she is going to make it. And you know I have always wanted to move and live somewhere else. To travel the world. I'm 28 today and what do I have to show for it? And I don't know, I like Jack. There's something about him, I can't explain what it is."

Joz is silent next to me. I am not sure what to say next or even if I should say anything at all. So instead, I lay as still as I can, afraid that if I move or make any sound, it will only cause her to continue to disagree with me. "I don't know FiFi. I'm in Kansas City. That means something right?" The sadness in her voice pierces me to my core. "What if you stay another couple days instead of jumping straight to moving across the country with a stranger? Let a couple days turn into a couple weeks and then by the end of summer decide."

"Once again, Joz, you know just what to do."

"What can I say, it's a gift." She smirks as she gets up and heads back to her room to finish packing. As soon as the door closes, I pick up my phone and dial Jack's number to tell him my decision. But he must be busy because he does not answer. Rather than leave a voicemail with the good news, I decide I will send him a text asking to see him before I leave so I can tell him the good news in person. While I wait for Jack to respond, I finish packing my bags. Whether I stay in Alabama or not, I still have to leave the condo.

At the restaurant, the four of us follow the host to our table. I spot the large ship wheel clock hanging on the wall; 11:30 am. It has been two hours since I texted Jack and with each hour that passes without hearing from him, I rethink my decision more and more. Maybe this is all vacation blues talking. I could never uproot my life and run away with a man I have only just met.

Our usual meal topics of the latest celebrity gossip, or for Alice, world politics, is exchanged for reliving the highlights of the week. However, it does not take us long to go from laughing about memories at the bar to concern over the stranger who left us all those messages. There really is a killer here, we can only be thankful that whoever was leaving those messages was just playing a disgusting joke on us. But someone really did break in on Monday night and steal the scrapbook Joz made for me. The scrapbook is out there somewhere with pictures from my childhood. Knowing Joz, my whole life was recorded in that book.

"Well guys, it's almost 1:30. We should probably get the check and head to the airport." Alice stated.

"No, we can't go yet. We haven't given Fiona her presents yet." Eden stated, handing me a small bag.

After opening my gifts, a beautiful silver pendant bracelet and a new romance novel, I glance at my phone once more. Still no text or call from Jack. I suppose he changed his mind about asking me to stay with him. Maybe I should change my mind also and fly home with the girls, leaving Jack as a memory of the best birthday week.

Thirty minutes until our flight is to board, I still cannot shake the memory of Jack asking me to stay. There still has been no response from him, but what if he lost his phone or our signals are getting lost and I am not receiving his messages? I cannot leave Alabama without knowing for sure.

"Joz. I made my decision." She looks at me sternly without saying a word so I take that as my cue to continue. "I can't go home with you. Not yet at least. I have to see him again. If anything, I will take a later flight home. But I need to talk to him before I board that plane."

"I understand FiFi. Do what you have to do."

"Thank you Joz. I love you! I'll be sure to text you what happens and let you know when I am coming home." Turning my attention to Eden and Alice, "Hey guys, there's something I have to do before I head home. I'll see you back in Kansas City. Thank you both for coming this week, it has been the best birthday ever!" They immediately start questioning what I have to do and where I have to go. "Joz, can you explain for me? I have to run."

"Yes. Now go!" As I pick up my bags, I hear Joz holler, "Hey! Be careful sis, I love you!" I blow her a kiss and give her a wink before turning back and heading for the airport doors.

Outside the airport, I flag down the next available

Uber and give the driver Jack's address. To pass the long 15-minute drive to his place, I try calling him again. I have no idea if he will be home when I get there but it is the only place I know to go.

I jump out of the car as soon as the driver comes to a stop and grab my suitcase from the trunk. As soon as the car pulls away, I turn towards Jack's house and take a deep breath in. I am not sure what awaits me next, but there is only one way to find out. I walk up and knock on the front door. Jack does not answer but I know he is home because I hear music through the open windows.

Turning the door knob, I find it is unlocked. Before I step in, I call out for Jack, not wishing to surprise him but the music is too loud inside to hear anything. So, I walk inside and set my bags down next to the couch. Looking around for Jack and calling out his name a couple of more times, I notice a light seeping underneath a door in the kitchen. I open the door and see a set of stairs leading to another door. 'That's strange.' I think to myself. I assumed this was a pantry when I was here on Wednesday, anything besides a basement.

"Jack?" I hesitantly call out. I hear muffled sounds, coming from behind the second door. When I do not hear a response, I slowly walk down the steps. I feel my legs begin to shake with each step as images from the movie Split flash through my head. When I reach the end of the stairs, I hold my breath as I strain to listen to what is on the other side of the door. *'Brooklyn, my dear. Are you ready?'* Brooklyn? He has another woman in there. How could he? I ask myself, trying to hold back tears of betrayal. Steading my breath and the shaking of my arms, I slowly turn the knob and open the door.

I attempt to scream at the sight but my voice is deceiving me. All I can do is stand there and watch. Watch as Jack drives a knife into a crying woman, again and again. Sixteen times. When he takes a step back to admire his work, I see it. Right there on the woman's torso, the letters C.K.

The Colorado Killer? Jack? Can he really be the killer? All those men and women. The stranger who broke into our condo, who left us those notes and stalked us. The man who attacked and may have caused Charlotte's death. I try to gather myself enough to make a run for it before Jack sees me but when I step back into the stairwell, I hit the door, causing it to creak open more. But this time, there are no screams to mask the sound. I look up and I see Jack staring back at me. His eyes gone cold and absent, bringing me back to the Jack who had sex with me the first time. The signs were there all along.

"J- Jack." I whimper.

CHAPTER 13: THE COLORADO KILLER

Saturday, June 20

Standing there, staring into Fiona's eyes, I see pain and betrayal. But it does not give me the same satisfaction as all those others have. Before, I would do anything to watch the hope leave their eyes. But now, here seeing the pain in Fiona's eyes, I feel nothing. *'How did we get here?'* I think to myself. She was never supposed to see this side of me. I was prepared to give it all up for her and never think about the thrill again. *'So how did we get here?'*

Earlier this morning in the shower, my thoughts went to Fiona and my proposal for her to stay. Since I did not hear from her last night, I took her silence as an answer. Within seconds, the fury surged through me like a wave. I knew the only way I was going to calm the rage was through teaching the beautiful brunette in my wine cellar a lesson.

Opening the basement door, I had no plan of letting Brooklyn live another day. Normally, I would start our sessions slow and gain intensity, but not today. Once I flip on the lights, I head straight for the water pitcher. Waterboarding her, I make sure to get as much of her wet as I can before pouring the rest of the water in a puddle at her feet. The best part is seeing her eyes when I picked up the cattle prod. She knew what was coming next and she knew there was no escape. *'She's almost ready.'* I thought to myself.

"Brooklyn, my dear, are you still with us?" Her head slumped down while her breathing became more shallow from the electrocution. "I hate to tell you, but you're not ready just yet. But how about this, I will let you rest for a bit and then later this afternoon, we can finish." I set the prod down on the counter, taking one last look at Brooklyn's limp body before I turned the lights off and headed upstairs.

I refilled my coffee for the third time and sat down at the kitchen table. Taking a deep breath in, I tried to slow the fury that still filled me. When I opened my eyes, I spotted the Sunday paper on the table with me as the headlines. I knew carving C.K would make Laine a kill to remember. Although the dimwits at the paper didn't appreciate the kill tag. Reaching to read my article again, I noticed the scrapbook that I stole from Fiona's on Monday. Only making my anger return with a vengeance once again. It may have been 8 o'clock in the morning but it was about time to trade the sugar in my coffee for Bailey's. A couple more cups and I will no longer feel a thing.

After I woke up from my late morning drunken nap, I could not help but wonder if Fiona had called, if only I could have remembered where I put my phone. Rather than look for it and be reminded of my disappointment, I headed back downstairs to finish Brooklyn.

When I looked into her eyes, I knew it was time. The hope had disappeared, replaced by sadness and fear. "Not much longer my dear. It's time now." I told her, picking up the knife to carve my new signature into her torso. Although she had exhausted herself, she still managed to scream and cry with each stab. After the 16th stab, I took a good long look at my newest masterpiece. Until I heard the creak of the door.

And now, here I stand, staring into the eyes of Fiona. Why is she even standing in my wine cellar in the first place?

"J-Jack?"

"Fiona-"

"Wha- Wh- Who is that? Jack, why?" Fiona stumbles over her questions as she continues to try to back into the stairwell.

"Fiona, I can explain. This, it's not what it looks like." I try to tell her, knowing full well it is exactly what it looks like.

When she turns to make a run up the stairs, I lunge after her. My fingers get a grip of one of her sandals, pulling her down onto the stairs before her shoe rips off and lets her crawl up the stairs out of my reach. I have to stop her, to explain to her. She cannot leave this house. I catch up to Fiona just in time as she reaches the top of the stairwell. Grabbing her exposed ankle, I squeeze tighter this time.

CHAPTER 14: JOZLYNN

Sunday, June 21

"Excuse me," I ask the hotel concierge as I approach the desk. "Can you show me how to get to Shoreline Bar from here?"

As Fiona's older sister, I knew I could not leave her alone in Alabama until I knew she was sure of her decision to stay. She should not have to experience any disappointment alone. Especially not on her birthday. This last year was disappointing enough for her.

When I checked into the hotel last night, I ordered a pizza, found Jumanji on T.V., pulled out my cell phone and waited for Fiona to call. But it never came.

I woke up 15 minutes till 9:00 AM; later than I had hoped. I shot up and grabbed my phone, expecting a text or call from Fiona checking in. Yet the only texts I have waiting for me are from Alice letting me know they made it home and an ex- co-worker asking if I was interested in having my job back. Neither of which are important if I do not hear from Fiona soon. I dial Fiona again and for the fifth time, got her voicemail. If I was not worried last night, I sure am this morning. This is not like her to not check in with me. Especially when it comes to a huge life decision like choosing to stay in a state 900-miles away with a guy she just met.

I had to think, *'where could she be?'* Sitting down on my hotel bed, I thought back on all Fiona had told me about this Jack guy while eating the omelet room service brought me for brunch. I remember her going on and on about this bar they went to after hours but could not recall the name of it. And then I remembered it was where that busboy found the woman's body. Searching on my phone, I found the news article on the Colorado Killer's latest victim and saw a photo of Shoreline Bar. I was not sure if FIona would be there, but it had to be as good of a place as any to start. Maybe they saw Fiona last night or can at least point me in the right direction of Jack's house. I quickly got dressed and headed downstairs to begin my search.

"Of course Miss." The concierge proceeds to give me step by step directions, not failing to mention that this route will take me past *'the most photogenic views around these parts.'* I do not have the heart to tell him that the views are the last thing on my mind so I simply thank him and head on my way, praying that I do not forget any of the turns.

Roughly 15 minutes later, I am walking into the Shoreline Bar at the peak of the lunch hour. I never did see Jack in person so I do not have the slightest clue who I am looking for. He could be any number of the men here. Making my way through the crowd to the bar, I get the bartender's attention, "Excuse me, Miss."

"Be right with ya." the bartender responds. Minutes later, she walks over to me and asks, "What can I get ya?"

"So this may seem an odd question, but I was wondering if Jack was working today?"

"Who?"

"Jack. I'm not sure his last name but he works here. A bartender I think. Darker hair, kind of lengthy."

"I'm sorry Miss, but I think this guy is pulling your leg. I don't know any Jacks here."

She must be mistaken, Fiona was positive Jack was a bartender at the same bar where the body was found. "Are you sure? Maybe he goes by Jackson at work? It's very important that I find him. I'm hoping he can tell me where my sister is."

She looks at me, sympathetic but partially annoyed

that I will not take no for an answer. "Hey Sam." She hollers across the room to a waiter walking by. "Do we have a Jack that works here? This woman thinks he's a bartender here."

"A Jack?" The waiter looks just as confused as the bartender. "Oh you know what, that one weird, quiet guy. Isn't his name Jack or John or something? Yeah, um-" He trails off thinking for a moment before speaking again with the snap of his finger. "Jack Thompson."

Finally, a last name. Now I am on to something. "You wouldn't happen to know where he lives would you? Or at least point me in the right direction?" The waiter looks disturbed by my question so before he can respond, I quickly explain how I am really looking for my sister and how I think she is with him.

"I'm sorry ma'am but we can't give out employee information like that. If your sister is missing, you should call the police."

"She's not missing per se. She's just not answering her phone. I don't want to involve the cops and make a big deal out of this."

I do not know if the waiter felt sorry for me or just wanted me to quit disrupting the lunch crowd, but he walks up to me, and in a hushed voice says, "Look, I don't know his exact address. And I couldn't give it to you if I did, but I will tell you, the views along the beach are beautiful this time of day. Maybe take a right out of here and enjoy a nice walk."

A direction is better than nothing I suppose. I thank the waiter for his advice and head on my way again, turning right when I reach the sand. Within minutes, I am no longer passing by bars, restaurants, and shops, rather I begin to see shacks. And the further I walk, the more abandoned the houses look. It feels like I have been walking for miles and I am about to turn around when I see a house set back aways and obscured by tall weeds. There is something curious about this one. Whereas the other houses this far down seem abandoned, this particular house, although still impersonal, looks as if someone has lived here recently. I walk further down the path to get a better look and notice the front door is swung open but there is no one around. Just to be safe, I kneel down and take a look around. I slowly creep closer and see a dark smear on the patio coming from the front door, down the porch stairs, to the grassy sand. I'm hoping it is only the shade from the sun, but from where I am crouching in the weeds, the smear has a red tint like blood.

All the possible worst case scenarios flash through my head; drowning out the possibilities that it could be an oil stain or the chance that I made the wrong turn somewhere along the way. But I cannot turn back until I know for sure. I take in one last look to ensure the homeowner will not sneak up on me while I check out the strange stain on the porch. When I am sure I am alone, I make a run for the house and stop just short of the front step. To my dismay, the stain is more red than I initially thought. *'Please Fiona! Don't be in here.'*

Before I can stop myself, I walk through the door. Inside is even more chilling than the smear of blood on the porch. My breath catches in my throat and my heartbeat quickens. I feel crazy as I swear the hair on the back of my neck stands up as chills run down my spine. Blood splattered on the walls, furniture pushed into the others, table lamps smashed on the floors. A view straight out of one of those horror films. I walk further into the house and sift through the papers and mail on the table to get a better idea of who lives here and what horrible thing happened. The first piece of mail I pick up I see his name; a water bill addressed to Jack Thompson. So I am at the right house but it does not give me any peace of mind.

Within seconds, my heartbeat stops when I see it. Sitting right there on the kitchen table, opened to her 16th birthday, the scrapbook that I made for Fiona. This is the home of the stranger who broke into our condo Monday night. The same stranger who left the rotten fish, sent us those pictures, and was watching us from our patio. All along, we thought it was a stranger or some sick prank. But this entire time, it was Jack, the man Fiona was seeing. The man Fiona stayed behind for.

'*Wait!*' I saw the newspapers laying next to the scrapbook and read the headlines. Each one was about the Colorado Killer. The connections came in such a wave it almost brought me to my knees. '*The C.K. written on our door, the woman's body left at the bar, Fiona's friend Charlotte. It's all connected.*' "Fiona, what have I done?" I ask aloud, my voice echoing through the house.

I cannot take it anymore. I have to get out of this house. The home of the Colorado Killer. No matter how many times I say it, it still does not seem possible. I step back on my heel and turn, making a run for the front door. Once I reach the grassy sand, my body can no longer take the gruesome stress. I hunch over and puke up everything. The omelet, the pizza, I do not stop until my body dry heaves with nothing left. Sobbing, I fall to the ground. Once my body is dried of bile and tears, I stand. "I'm going to find you Fiona." I confidently promise the wind. '*I have to. One way or another.*' This time, I make the promise to myself, a little less confident in what exactly I will find.

I walk back to the porch and like a coonhound, I find my trail and follow the smear of blood. I lose sight of the trail through the thicker weeds but I take my best guess and keep walking forward. Now that I am walking with no clues, I scan every inch of the horizon. I can only hope he did not throw her out to sea to be lost forever.

I have been searching for hours with no sign of Fiona or Jack. About to turn back and start from the beginning, I hear muffled sounds coming from the other side of some large rocks. I carefully climb up one of the rocks and slowly peek my head over to see where the sound is coming from. About another mile up, there is a hoard of people on the beach. Just as I am climbing over the rocks, I see police arrive on the beach and begin escorting the tourists back. My heart sank, there lying on the beach, is a motionless body. "Fiona?" I manage to whimper.

As I approach the scene I push through all the onlookers to get a better look. Catching my breath when I finally made my way to the police tape. It is not her. It is not Fiona. I have never seen this woman before but she is some preppy looking blonde. Before the Medical Examiner could cover her body, I saw the letters C.K. carved into her abdomen among all the stab wounds. This has to be the blood I saw coming from the house. Fiona has to be safe somewhere, hiding from Jack. I have to find her first.

I turn around and swim upstream out of the crowd. I begin to head back towards the house to see if I missed any clues about where Fiona could be and why she has not called me. I am halfway to the large rocks that separate the tourist beach from the abandoned houses when I look over and see a large orange object between two of the rocks. As I walk closer, my pace slows as I begin to make out the object is not an object at all. It is a woman with brunette hair covering her face, wearing an orange dress and a silver bracelet glistening in the sunlight.

"Fiona?" I scream as I run to the body. Brushing the bloody hair from her eyes, I let out a loud cry as Fiona's lifeless eyes stare back into mine. "HELP!" I scream as loud as I can, trying to get the attention of the police. But no one comes, so I am left alone, sobbing over my sister's dead body. "Fiona, I'm so sorry. I should not have let you go alone. How did I let this happen?"

I hear the commotion from the detectives begin to die down so I look over and see the Medical Examiner wheeling the body away and the crime scene detectives packing up. "Fiona? I have to go. I need to go get the detective and bring them to you. But I'll be right back, I promise." Standing, I take one last look at her before walking back towards the detectives.

Before I head to the police station to answer the detectives' questions, I stop by my hotel room. There are only two people I know of who crossed paths with The Colorado Killer and survived. Picking up my cell phone, I find the number for the Ridgeview hospital and ask for Charlotte Hearon.

"Hi, um, is this Charlotte Hearon's room?"

"Yes it is. Who is this?" A husky voice responds.

"This is Jozlynn. I'm not sure Charlotte knows me but she is, or was friends, I don't really know. But she knows my sister, Fiona. Fiona Lewis." I ramble back. I have no idea what I am going to say but I know Charlotte will know what I should do.

"Listen," he pauses. "Charlotte has been in a coma for almost three months now and she just woke up a few days ago. I don't think now is the best time to bring up any unnecessary stress for her. I'm sorry but you'll have to call back."

"No wait!" I plead before he hangs up. "Is this Liam? Fiona called on Thursday and talked to you, didn't she?"

"What is this about? Is everything okay? She called saying she thought the Colorado Killer was stalking her but I have not had a chance to call back to check in." I could not speak. "Hello? Jozlynn, are you still there?"

"He killed her." The words come out impersonal "My sister is dead." It was the first time I said those words.

"Jozlynn, I am so sorry. I didn't-" He was interrupted by a female voice that I can only assume is Charlotte.

"Hello, Jozlynn? This is Charlotte. Please tell me Fiona is alright!"

The only response I can give her are uncontrollable sobs. When I finally gain my voice back, I tell her what I told Liam. "The Colorado Killer, he got her." She stops me before I can continue so we can move this conversation to her cell phone and I can be put on speaker to talk to both Charlotte and Liam.

After I replay the entire week for them, we all sit there in silence for a moment until I speak up again. "Now the detectives want me to come in to tell them what I know. I mean, I can take them to his house where he killed her. I can show them the scrapbook he stole. But what if the police don't do anything? He cannot get away with this!"

"Jozlynn, what are you going to do?" Charlotte asks innocently.

"I'm going to do what I need too." I am not sure what this is exactly but I know it is not me going to the station. Fiona deserves more than a long drawn out court hearing resulting in her killer getting a cozy bed and three meals a day. If he is going to pay for all those people he killed, I will have to do it myself.

CHAPTER 15: THE COLORADO KILLER

Sunday, June 21

After positioning Fiona's body against the rocks, I come back and take Brooklyn's body further onto the beach. I want my work displayed but Fiona was not meant to be number 17. It was rather sloppy, probably the most sloppy I have been, so I chose not to tag her as mine.

Pacing my kitchen, careful not to step on any of the broken glass, I force myself to think. *'Why did she have to show up when she did. We could have avoided all of this if only she did not see me in the wine cellar.'*

I cannot take it in this house any longer. Fiona's blood splatter on the walls reflecting my mistake and clouding my logical thinking. Taking a walk seems to be the only way I will clear my head so I head out towards the beach, not bothering to shut the door behind me.

About 10-minutes into my walk, I start to feel like myself again. Emotions are no longer driving my thoughts, rather I am beginning to be able to think of Fiona as any other kill. As I circle back to the house, I decide to take the scenic route along the beach and see if anyone has come across my masterpiece. And there they are, the red and blue lights, detectives covering the beach, police tape blocking off the area, and best of all, the fear in the eyes of the onlookers. Taking it all in, I pan over to where I left Fiona. I did not expect anyone to notice her right away, giving me time to think about what to do next. But, crouching over Fiona's body is a woman. I squint to see further and notice the woman is her sister Jozlynn. I only met her once but from my week of watching them, I have no doubt it is her.

"Shit." I mutter under my breath. Her sister was supposed to be back in Kansas City by now. She must have stayed back with Fiona. If she stayed, she must know Fiona came looking for me last night. And now, she must know that I am the one that killed Fiona. "Shit." I mutter again. None of this was supposed to happen. It will not be long now before Jozlynn tells the police about me and they come looking for me at home. And when they arrive, they will see the blood stains and the broken glass everywhere. *'I have to get out of here. Now!'* I tell myself as I make a run for the house to pack as much as I can and hit the road.

This is the closest I have ever come to getting caught. It is only a matter of time before the FBI shows up at my door and hauls me in. And I am not ready to call it quits yet. Definitely not like this. When I stop, it will be on my own terms.

I take a couple of bags to the car and swear I saw a shadow duck behind the weeds. I must be paranoid now but I do not want to take any chances. Only one more arm load of bags and the rest I will have to leave behind.

Back inside, I must choose between my wood carvings and my books. As I'm weighing the decision, a tapping sound comes from one of the living room windows. I snap my head around to see what was causing the noise but before I could take a step towards the window, whatever it was begins tapping on the other living room window. And then on the kitchen window, and then the back door. Whatever is making that sound is surrounding me.

"Oh J-Ack." A voice whispers through the cracked kitchen window. "I ssseee yoouu."

"Who's there?" I demand.

"I know who you are." The voice, a woman's voice, is moving back around the house. Any worry I had dissipates. I can handle a woman.

"What do you want?"

"I know what you did." This time the voice is coming from the front porch.

I square my body to face the front door, prepared for whoever walks in. "Then come in and face me."

"You're the Colorado Killer. And you're about to die."

THE COLORADO KILLER

Friday, October 16

A fall in Idaho is more beautiful than I imagined. As I sit in my new cabin, sipping coffee on the porch overlooking the Teton Mountains, I think back to my time in Alabama, to Fiona. Her cold eyes haunt me every time I close my eyes. But the memories of the kill thrill me.

I have lived here for almost four months now and I am not disappointed. The sights alone fill me with a feeling of tranquility. The hues of the trees, oranges and reds, against the bright blue of the sky. The mountains in the distance and the sound of the river rushing by up ahead. This is the perfect place for my next exploit. Now all is left is to lure my next victims across the country to the quaint town of Evans, Idaho.

Fiona's death was a mistake. I am no longer blaming myself but there is a list of people who did her wrong and led to her death. Starting with her Father. He left his only family when Fiona was just a little girl, leaving her to sort out the abandonment of the one man she looked up to. And then there is Sawyer. The prick who left her shortly after their trip to the Cayman Islands for a blonde bimbo. You cannot forget about Liam. Fiona knew something was wrong and the one man she reached out to hung up on her. If any of these men would have treated Fiona the way she deserved to be treated, I fully believe she would still be alive. And now, they will pay.

'But how can I get them to come to me?' It only took me a couple weeks to decide on Idaho. After driving north from Orange Beach I made some stops, Nashville, Fayetteville, Salt Lake City, but none of them felt right. Then when I was in Green River, Wyoming, I remembered Fiona telling me about Idaho and how she always dreamt of visiting the Teton Mountains and Yellowstone someday. And what better way to honor her memory when killing her enemies than in a place she dreamt about.

Over the last three months, I have had plenty of time to plan my revenge. I spent many hours researching my targets, digging up any dirt I could find. Now it is time to execute.

I stand up, taking in a deep breath of the peaceful

air before it is gone, and head to my kitchen where three large envelopes lay. One for each of my targets. Inside each envelope contains details and photos of private affairs they would not want released to the public. Affairs such as shady business deals, identity fraud, and well, affairs. I also included a letter letting each man know that I am not after their money. I simply want to invite them to a week in Idaho where after, I will make all this disappear for good. Where even the FBI cannot trace it.

Grabbing the envelopes, I jump in my car and head to the local post office. I can only hope Janet is not working today. She is always nosey, reading the shipping address of every piece of mail you send. When these three men arrive in town, and worse, are found dead, I do not need Janet blabbing her mouth that she assisted me in luring them here.

'Whew!' I release the breath I am holding in as I open the door to see Michael standing behind the counter. Michael just graduated from High School five months ago and instead of going to college, he is stuck in this small town earning money to send his little sister to college in two years. Needless to say, he could not care less about who you are or what you are mailing.

" Let the games begin." I say aloud after watching Michael throw the envelopes in the bag for processing. Just a few more days and my targets will receive my gifts and come running to Evans.

BOOKS IN THIS SERIES

The Colorado Killer